FALL OF DARKNESS

Survive the Darkness Book 9

RYAN CASEY

Oliver Pritchard collapsed to the road, and he knew he wasn't going to get back up again.

Rain pelted down heavily from above, drenching him. He was already soaked as fuck, so it didn't make much difference, really. It was late morning. But it could be late afternoon with how dark it was. Thick grey skies above. Felt like the sun was never going to show its face again.

Fitting, in a way.

Because it pretty much summed up how Oliver felt about everything.

He watched the rain pour down the overflowing gutters on the street at the side of him. Just a normal street. Nothing distinctive about it.

Only that wasn't true, was it?

Because there was no such thing as a "normal street" anymore.

Especially not with the bodies lying on the pavement.

He saw them, and he felt strong vomit creeping up his throat. A woman and a man lying face flat on the pavement. Someone had thrown a black bin bag over the pair of them to try and cover them up. But that bin bag had fallen free now.

And as Oliver lay there, he could see the face of the man staring back at him.

Staring at him with those wide, haunted eyes.

With that grey face.

He looked into those eyes, and he saw himself reflected in them.

This would be him soon.

This would be him.

He listened to the rain hammering down all around him. He used to find that sound soothing. Used to like sitting in the living room, football on, looking out at the street as it filled with rain. He could hear Billy upstairs, playing on his video games. And that annoyed him. Sure, he loved his video games just as much as Billy did.

But he wanted Billy to be out in the rain like the other kids were, splashing around. Playing on their bikes. Not a care in the world about the weather.

He wanted Billy to be tougher.

Stronger.

He thought about Billy, and his stomach sank. He didn't know where he was. He'd tried looking for him. Tried searching for him for weeks now. He'd tried home. He'd tried family. He'd tried relatives, and he'd tried friends.

But there was no trace of him.

There was no sign of him.

And now here he was.

He lay there, face flat on the road. The rotting smell of those bodies on the pavement kept drifting towards him, filling his nostrils, and making him want to vomit. He'd smelled some smells since the power went out a month or so ago. Some real nasty smells. And he'd seen some awful sights, too. Looting. Violence. Murder.

But this...

There was something about this smell that really got to him more than any of that.

Because it was intertwined with thoughts about Billy.

Thoughts about his boy.

He thought about Kyla. Thought about how guilty he was for what he'd done to her. For the affair he'd had.

And maybe that was part of why he was out here now.

Even though he knew where she was.

Even though she was back home. Probably waking up right now and wondering where the hell he was at.

Part of this was guilt for how he'd spent New Year.

For the affair he'd been having.

But then...

Another thought shot into his mind.

Billy.

Kyla.

The gut-wrenching truth about everything.

No. Don't think that. Don't you go there. You don't have to go there...

He pushed that thought away. Pushed it to one side.

Because he didn't want to think about that.

He didn't need to think about that.

He just had to focus on now.

Right now.

And right now...

There was no sign of Billy.

And he was lost.

And he didn't know how much he had left in the tank.

He lay there, face flat. And he waited for whatever fate awaited him. He thought about Billy. Thought about how he'd always wanted to toughen him up. How he'd always wanted him to do sporty things, like football and like rugby. How he'd always tried to push him and encourage him.

Bully him, more like.

He shook his head at that. No. That wasn't true. He'd never bullied his son. He would never do such a thing.

But...

No.

No, don't think about the "but".

Push the "but" away.

It's too dangerous to think about.

Too dangerous to process.

He thought about Billy, and he thought about Kyla, and he thought about how he wanted his family back together.

Because in this world... things could be different.

In this world, things could be better.

He thought about them both as he drifted off into exhaustion and unconsciousness.

As he felt the rain turning from cold to warmth.

As the smell of rot turned to the smell of sweetness.

As everything felt good again, just for a moment.

And then he took a deep breath and went to drift off into this bliss.

That's when he heard something.

Something right ahead of him.

Footsteps.

He looked up.

Saw them standing there.

Saw the figures standing before him.

Staring down at him.

Wordless.

Speechless.

A woman leading them.

Totally still.

She walked up to him.

Stood over him.

Her silhouette blocking the sunlight.

She stood over him for God knows how long. What did she

want? Who the hell was she? Was she even real or a figment of Oliver's imagination?

He was about to open his mouth and say something when she finally spoke.

"You look like you need a hand," she said.

Oliver didn't know it then. He didn't understand the significance then.

But that was the moment everything changed.

CHAPTER TWO

"I'm really not sure about this, Billy."

"Well, I am."

"I get that. I appreciate why you're doing this. I understand why you want to do it. But—"

"You don't have to come with me."

"What?"

"I said... I said you don't have to come with me. I can go on my own. If you want."

"Get real, kid. That ain't gonna happen."

"Then stop moaning about it."

"Wow. You're really getting a bit of confidence, aren't you?"

"You like it?"

"Honestly, I'm not entirely sure."

Billy looked at his old school up ahead. It was exactly as he remembered it. Only... quieter. Usually, he heard children laughing and screaming. The bell ringing, and the kids all racing to line up and go back inside. Dinner ladies walking around on lunch duty like prison guards, making sure nobody was pushing their luck, being naughty.

And he could feel it. If he really concentrated, really focused, he could feel it all again. Feel like he was back there five years ago. He never really enjoyed school. Didn't have many friends. Got picked on and teased a little by the other kids for being "weak." Even his dad used to tell him he needed to "toughen up."

He wished it was as simple as flicking a switch and toughening up; he really did.

But what he'd give to be back here. What he'd give for another chance to do it all again.

Because the scariness of school was nothing compared to the world he'd lived in these last few years.

Right now, as much as his school hadn't changed much to look at... it *felt* different.

That silence. That quietness. It felt empty. It felt haunted. There were skipping ropes lying in the middle of the play area. Hopscotch games gone unfinished. Cars still filled up the car park at the front, covered in rust and dust. Loads of rides filled the car park and the fields, too, there from the New Year's fair they always used to have here. Ferris wheels. Merry-go-rounds. And those rides that spun people around in the air, so, so high.

He didn't want to look too closely at the skeletons still trapped inside the clutches of those rides.

People who'd never got out.

"I just don't like it," Kayleigh said. "Whole place gives me the creeps."

Billy looked at her. Saw her staring at the school with narrowed eyes. Her blonde hair looked dirty. Her skin was pale. She looked like she hadn't smiled in a long, long time.

Rex stood between them, wagging his tail. He didn't seem that bothered about any of this.

"It's like I said—"

"I'm not leaving you, you idiot," Kayleigh said.

"But if you don't like it here, I understand if you—"

"I made a promise a month ago," Kayleigh said. "I intend to keep it."

I made a promise.

A knot tightened in Billy's stomach.

A vice tensed around his chest.

Billy knew exactly who Kayleigh was talking about.

The moment she was referring to.

He still felt sad about it all the time.

The bond he'd formed. The connection he'd made.

How much he missed her.

But he didn't have time to think about it right now.

Kayleigh sighed. "Look. We do a quick sweep. Chances are the locks've already been broken. But we can't stay there long. There's... there'll be nothing here for you. I don't even know *why* you're back here. Not really. There's nothing left here."

"But maybe there will be something."

She opened her mouth. Looked like she was going to argue for a second. Then sighed and shook her head. "Aoife never told me how stubborn you were."

"Is that a yes?"

Kayleigh shrugged. She looked around. Looked at this silent school yard. Ahead, crows cawed, cutting through the silence with their echoing calls. "I guess you're not leaving me with much choice—"

"Good. Then let's go."

He walked down the pathway right towards the main entrance, which used to be reserved for adults and teachers or if you'd been naughty and Mr Franklin wanted to see you. He felt quite big, walking across these cracked flags, over to that door. The last time he'd been through this way, it was when Wayne got him in trouble for smashing a window, even though it wasn't him who'd done it.

He was always getting in trouble for things he hadn't done.

Just too weak to stand up for himself.

He walked towards that door. The windows here were smashed. The doors looked rusty. The whole place looked like it was falling to bits. The roof probably wouldn't be safe. Kids used to climb up and sit up there at weekends. He'd done enough falling through roofs to last a lifetime since the power had gone out.

He grabbed the rusting handle to the main entrance. Looked up at Kayleigh.

She didn't say anything. Just rolled her eyes and shrugged.

He had to take that as permission to enter.

He pulled the handle.

And to his surprise, the door opened.

He was immediately met with the stench of dampness. The air was dusty and made him cough. Everything was echoey. He swore he saw something move up ahead, in the corner of the reception area and realised it was probably mice or rats. Made him shiver a little. Still didn't like rodents. Still scared him. Even in a world where he'd been through so many horrors, it was the old night-mares that got to him.

"Eyes ahead," Kayleigh said. "The sooner we get out of this creep hole, the better."

Billy walked past the reception area, where the admin people used to sit; the people you had to speak to if you felt sick and wanted to go home early, something he'd faked a few times. He pretended he had tummy ache, but really he just didn't want to have to spend any more time being picked on or teased. And he felt like the reception people knew this, too. So they went easier on him than they did the other kids. Helped that his Auntie Karen used to work on reception, too. She wasn't his real auntie. One of those aunties you call auntie for reasons nobody can ever explain.

Everyone has an auntie who isn't really their auntie, right?

He walked through the big double doors and into the corridor that led its way past the classrooms towards the assembly hall.

He saw his old reception class. Saw the books on the floor, the bean bags sitting there. The whiteboard, with little smiley face drawings on it.

He saw the sandpit in the corridor. The Scalextric set. He saw so many reminders of how things used to be. Paintings on the walls, some of them by his old classmates. Smiling faces in blood-red ink.

He saw them all, and he felt himself smiling. Felt a tear rolling down his face.

"Remind me exactly why we're here again?" Kayleigh asked.

Billy's stomach turned.

Why was he really here?

He wasn't sure. He couldn't explain it.

Only... he felt like he needed something from the past.

He felt like he needed family.

He felt weak without them.

"My auntie," Billy said. "She used to—"

"Work here. Yeah. I remember you saying. Only... slight problem. The blackout happened at New Year's Eve. Why the hell would she be in school at midnight on New Year's Eve?"

Damn it. That was a good point and one he'd not thought of.

"The fair," he said, looking down, his cheeks burning. "She—she was helping out at the fair."

It was a fair excuse, he thought. A lie. But a fair excuse.

And yet he couldn't escape Kayleigh's judgemental stare.

"Why are we really here, Billy?"

He looked up at her, and he wanted to tell her the truth. He wanted to tell her everything. He wanted to tell her exactly how he was feeling.

And then he heard something.

Movement.

Footsteps.

In the dinner hall.

He froze.

There was someone in there.

There was someone in there, and he had to go look.

He had to go investigate.

It could be someone he knew.

He turned around and walked towards the hall right away.

"Billy," Kayleigh said.

But Billy wasn't stopping. He couldn't stop.

Because maybe someone was here.

Maybe one of his old teachers was here.

Or someone he used to go to school with.

Or Auntie Karen.

Or even...

Mum or Dad?

No. Why would they be here?

Why wouldn't they be here?

"Billy!" Kayleigh called.

He reached the dining hall and opened the doors when he saw exactly what made the noise.

A bunch of pigeons strutted around in the middle of the old dining hall. The dark wood, which doubled as a P.E. hall, was covered in...

He smelled it. Smelled it in the air, so sour, so unmistakable, and he knew.

He knew exactly what it was.

Death.

"Billy," Kayleigh said. "We... we have to get out of here. There's nothing for us here."

He looked across the hall. Looked at the water dripping down from the gap on the open roof above. Saw the sweet stalls they put on inside during the New Year fair, all lying on their side. A sickly stench of decaying sugar hanging in the air. Weeds and foliage sprouting up everywhere.

He saw the old gym equipment dangling from the ceilings. The ropes he used to hate trying to climb up. Still filled him with fear now.

He saw the piano that Mrs Crawton used to sit at and play while they were singing hymns. Half of the keys had been torn away, and there was a hole in the side of the wood, bird shit spilling out of it.

And in the middle of the hall, he saw something else.

Something that filled him with even more fear.

Three bodies.

Three children.

Skeletons.

Skeletons that the rats and the birds were picking at.

"There's nothing here for us," Kayleigh said. "I'm sorry, kiddo."

He stood there, and he felt this weakness. He felt like a failure.

Because those little skeletons could be kids he once knew.

And they were gone now.

They were gone, just like everyone else.

He looked at the hall that used to feel so comfortable. Looked at where he used to sit during assembly, singing hymns and Mr Prittesh's silly Monkeys Eat Bananas song.

He looked at where Jason Welsh did a big poo in the middle of assembly and sent the whole school into chaos.

He looked at it all, and he felt so lost, and he felt so sad.

"We'd better... Billy?"

He didn't stop for anything or anyone.

He just turned around, stepped out of the dining hall, and he ran.

CHAPTER THREE

"You really shouldn't run away like that."

The second Billy heard Kayleigh's voice right behind him, he sighed. He knew he shouldn't be stroppy with her. She just cared about him. Worried about him. Well, that's what she said, anyway. But really, he could tell she wasn't as keen on him as Aoife used to be. He didn't get on with her as well as he got on with Aoife. They didn't have a connection like he'd had with her.

He just felt... lost. Like he didn't know where to go. Like he was looking for something—family, friends, anything from his past.

He didn't know why it'd all just come back to haunt him lately. Since Aoife died.

But then... that was it, wasn't it?

He'd spent so long in Ramiro's captivity that he hadn't even had the time or the chance to really go looking for something that felt like home again.

He thought Aoife was the family and the home he was looking for.

But now she was gone.

And he was stuck with Kayleigh, who... he didn't like as much. As bad as he felt for thinking that. But he was pretty sure she wasn't massively keen on him either.

It was getting dark. He didn't like night-time. Kayleigh always wanted to stop and rest at night-time, but he wanted to keep on going. Keep on walking. Keep on searching.

And at times, he felt like he was with Aoife again. Back with Aoife when she didn't want to find people; didn't want to find any communities for them to become a part of. Because she was scared.

But he knew things were different with Kayleigh.

He didn't like to admit it, but he knew Kayleigh was just more... realistic.

And that scared him.

The wind was cool but not as icy as it had been. It must be spring now. The buds were coming out on the trees. A month since they'd lost Aoife, and the last of the snow was already melting at that point.

He used to love it when it was getting closer to summer when he was younger. The thought that he'd have all that time off school to play on his Xbox, to kick his football around his garden. Dad used to tell him to go down to the park on his bike and play with his friends. But Billy didn't really like cycling. It scared him. Embarrassed him to admit it and embarrassed Dad to hear it, but it did.

He'd rather just spend the time at home. Curtains closed, the smell of the warm air creeping inside. Just him and his Xbox.

A life he missed.

"I'm just looking out for you, lad," Kayleigh said, panting along, Rex trailing behind them, sniffing at some dead animal or other. "This whole trek back down memory lane... it's not been good for you. Seriously. I know it too well myself."

He looked up at Kayleigh. Saw her staring ahead, down the road they were on. It was just a normal street near the front of his old school. Houses all the way down. Up ahead, there was a little pond with a play area, where Billy used to cut through to get home from school. Always got teased by the older kids smoking on benches as he walked through. He didn't know why. He didn't think there was anything particularly weird or different about him.

He figured he was just... weak. And they sensed that.

"I have to go home first," he said.

Kayleigh sighed. "Trust me. I'm not... I'm not convinced that's the best idea."

"Well, we're here. So I might as well."

Billy hadn't been home since the blackout began. He tried to find his way there but couldn't and then ended up with other people anyway. He didn't know what'd happened to Dad. What'd happened to Mum. He knew what'd happened to Grandma, and he didn't like to think about that...

But having not been back home... that was something that always bothered him. Always got to him.

He needed to see. He needed to get an idea of what'd happened.

And he just needed... *something*.

"I'm just saying," Kayleigh said. "I... I went home myself. Early on. And..."

She stopped. Her voice broke up. She looked away. Her cheeks were flushed.

"Are you okay?" Billy asked.

She looked back around at him, frowned. A hard look returning to her face. "Why wouldn't I be?"

Billy wanted to push her and ask her more.

But in the end, he didn't want to force her to speak about anything.

They didn't really get on. Kayleigh wasn't that talkative with him. She was different to Aoife. Colder, somehow. And it seemed like she was travelling with him because she felt she had to, because of what'd happened to Aoife. Because of the promise she'd made.

As much as he tried not to, as much as he strained to resist, he thought back to that day.

Back to Carlton.

He thought about Aoife as she lay there, holding on to Billy's hand.

He thought about the anger he'd felt and the sadness he'd felt.

If you'd acted stronger...

If only you'd not drawn her into your messy little life...

He pushed those thoughts away, shook his head.

"You know," Kayleigh said. "Aoife would be proud of you. If she saw how far you've come."

"You sound like you're going to say 'but'."

Kayleigh smiled. "Bingo."

"But what?"

"I just... I don't know. All this looking for your family. And before today. Looking for a place to go. Searching for some kind of connection and meaning out there. You're chasing ghosts, Billy. You're chasing ghosts because, for whatever reason, you don't feel strong enough as you are. And if you aren't careful... that'll catch up with you. You need to stop chasing ghosts."

Billy heard Kayleigh's words, and he felt that familiar sense of anger creeping up again. The anger he'd felt when he was standing over Carlton's body. Blood all over his hands. Rage filling every inch of his body.

"But hell. Why am I getting all philosophical with a kid?"

"What do you know about anything, anyway?" he said. He knew it was petty. But he was tired, and it was getting late, and it was another day of not getting anywhere at all.

Kayleigh's eyes widened. "Trust me. I know more than you think."

"But you didn't know how to save Aoife either, did you?"

She opened her mouth. Froze. Billy knew what he'd said was bad right away. And he felt bad about it. Guilty about it.

But he just felt so mad.

He just felt so lost.

He just felt so alone.

"I'll let that one go," Kayleigh said. "This once. But if you say anything like that again, you're on your own, kid. And then you'll be forced to grow the fuck up and stop chasing ghosts, once and for all."

She walked on, Rex close to her side. She sounded really upset.

"Now come on," she said, standing at the turn in the road, waiting for Billy. "Are we going to go back to your old pad or what? The sooner we get this shit done with, the better."

Billy stood there. He shouldn't have said that to Kayleigh.

But then she shouldn't have said what she said either.

You need to stop chasing ghosts.

He swallowed a lump in his throat, took a deep breath, and followed Kayleigh to the end of the street.

It was time to go back home.

And it was time to see what he could find.

But he couldn't get those words out of his head, and wondering.

You need to stop chasing ghosts...

CHAPTER FOUR

illy stood outside the gate leading to his house, and he felt like he was dreaming.

He'd visited home a lot in his thoughts and dreams. Particularly when he was with Ramiro and his people. He'd picture himself walking through the green front gate that Mum used to paint every year without fail. Walking up to the front door. Mum standing there with a big smile on her face. Dad ruffling his hair as Mum held him tight.

And he felt warm. He felt calm. He felt at peace.

He felt so, so happy.

He felt... well. *Home*.

But being here now... it was like being back at his old primary school. It felt different, somehow. It felt like he was stepping back into a place he barely recognised. Like aliens had come down and attempted to recreate his home from memory. Some things just didn't feel right. The mucky windows. The gate, rustier than usual, missing its annual repainting.

And the silence.

It just felt weird.

Because the things that made home "home" itself weren't here anymore—

No.

He couldn't think that way.

He didn't know that. Not for sure.

Not yet...

He closed his eyes, swallowed a lump in his throat. He had to stay calm. He was here. After all these years, all this time, he was back.

Home for Billy was a terraced house on what was once a busy street. But this street was so quiet now. It was like when they were doing the roadworks further down the street that time, so closed it to all traffic. Dad kept going on about how much nicer it was when there wasn't traffic going up and down it all the time.

Billy never really understood.

It didn't feel nice to him at all.

It felt lifeless.

It felt dead.

The grass in the front of the garden was tall and orange. It looked ancient. He saw the plants, too. Saw these little spikes of wood all around this front garden. Mum wouldn't be happy to see the state of them. She always looked after her plants and always loved her gardens. Billy never saw the fuss. They were just flowers, after all.

But now he understood. Seeing how lifeless it looked. Seeing how dead it looked.

It worried him.

It made him worried about what he was going to find inside...

No.

Don't think that way.

He looked at the lounge window. It looked dark inside. But at least the glass wasn't smashed. Damp and dirty and speckled with black mould but not smashed.

And then he looked upstairs.

Up at his mum and dad's bedroom window.

His stomach turned.

What was in there?

What was he going to find inside?

"You don't have to do this, you know," Kayleigh said.

Billy jumped back into reality. Looked around at Kayleigh. Saw her staring down at him. She looked like she was concerned. Like she was worried about him but was too afraid to say exactly why.

He looked back around at the rest of the street. At the usual sight of abandoned cars, all the way up the road.

And then at his front door.

"No," he said. "I do. I... I just do."

She looked like she wanted to say something to him. To stop him. To tell him this wasn't a good idea and that they should turn around and walk away or something like that.

But she didn't.

Instead, she just nodded. "Well, I'll be right here with you."

He took a deep breath.

His legs felt like jelly.

Be strong, Billy. Got to be strong.

As hard as it was, he walked.

He walked down the pathway and got a flashback to when he was coming home from school. The relief he always felt.

And yet...

That relief was short-lived, wasn't it?

Because he knew Dad would always be in a bad mood. And that he'd always tell him off for something.

But still. Anything was better than school, wasn't it?

He looked over to the right before he reached the front door. Looked over towards Steve's garden. Steve was a neighbour of theirs. He always seemed to be standing out there when Billy got home from school. Smile on his face. Dad didn't like him. Found him a bit weird. Told Billy not to speak with him.

But Billy thought he was okay.

Still. What Dad says goes…

He reached the front door. Stood right opposite it. Heart racing. Hands sweaty.

Here goes, Billy. Here goes…

He reached for the handle. Went to turn it.

The door didn't budge.

He sighed. Lowered his head. If it was locked, that meant… well, what did it mean?

"We could always try the window," Kayleigh said.

Billy looked at the window. He felt bad about breaking the window of his own home. But then, what other choice did he have?

He went to nod when he noticed something in front of the window, and he smiled.

He walked over. Lifted the plant pot, struggled to get it onto its side.

"Now's not the time for gardening," Kayleigh said, as Rex sniffed around, trying to get involved.

But this wasn't gardening.

He strained as hard as he could to lift the pot to one side.

Please be here. Please be here…

And then he saw it.

The spare key lying there on the ground.

His smile widened.

He grabbed the key. Dropped the plant pot in the process, which cracked everywhere. Woodlice and worms spilled out, something else Rex found particularly fascinating.

"Got it," Billy said.

Kayleigh shook her head. "Didn't have to make such a mess of it, did you?"

Billy ignored her and walked over to the door. He stuck the key in the lock with his shaking hand. Turned it. And he had visions of the key not fitting in 'cause there was one at the other side, something Mum always told Dad off for.

This has to be it. This has to work. Please, please work...

And it did.

It turned.

And then the door to Billy's home opened.

Right away, it was like stepping into a time machine.

It was dusty. So much dustier than it'd ever been when he was here.

And it smelled a bit... weird. Not the usual flowery smell that Mum always liked. Like something sour. Old milk.

But it was home.

It was home, just as he remembered it.

He looked around. Saw the leather sofa in the middle of the lounge that he used to always sit between Mum and Dad on to watch television. He saw his pile of DVDs over in the corner by the telly. He saw the photographs on the windowsill and the fireplace of him, Mum, and Dad. School photos. Holiday photos.

So many happy faces.

He wasn't sure how long he just stood there, soaking it all up. But what struck him more than anything was that he felt home again. He knew it sounded cheesy... but it was like he was a little boy again. Like he was looked after and cared for again. Like he was safe again.

And then he started coughing on the dust and smelled that mouldiness, and he realised this wasn't home as he'd remembered it at all.

He walked through to the kitchen. Saw two bowls on the little round table in the middle and a box of Corn Flakes in between. He saw the hamster cage at the far side of the room for Snowy, his pet.

A little excitement sparked in his belly. Snowy! He hadn't thought of Snowy in so, so long.

Maybe he'd be in there.

Maybe he'd be okay.

He ran across the kitchen, over towards him, and he saw it.

Smelled that sourness grow a little worse.

Then saw it lying there.

A little hamster skeleton amidst the brown sawdust.

Sadness sank over him. Poor Snowy. He must've been alone in here for so long. No food at all.

He saw the metal of the cage, worn down by his hamster's teeth, and he felt even worse.

He must've been trying to gnaw his way out.

He turned around, walked towards the back of the kitchen.

He saw the garden was overgrown. Saw that weeds were taking over, something Mum would hate.

He saw beetles creeping around the kitchen, and he realised that no matter how much it looked like an imitation or an impression of his old home... it wasn't it.

"You okay?" Kayleigh asked.

He ignored her and walked to the foot of the stairs.

He stood there. Looked up. He wasn't sure what he was expecting to find. Wasn't sure what he was hoping for at all. Finding Mum and Dad still here? He knew that was a long shot.

But...

Just something.

Just anything.

Just some kind of sign.

Some kind of hope.

He climbed the stairs. Dodged the third step like he always used to. Always thought stepping on that third step was unlucky for whatever reason he couldn't explain.

He reached the top of the stairs and looked to the left, into the bathroom.

The bath looked messy. Like something had died in there. And it smelled, too. Smelled really bad.

His toothbrush still sat in the cup next to Mum and Dad's. It looked brown and mouldy now.

He turned away, sighing.

Keep on going. Keep on going...

He walked over to the door opposite.

The door to Mum and Dad's room.

And as he stood there, just for a moment, he found himself praying.

Please. Please be home. Please, please give me a sign.

He pushed that door open.

Mum and Dad's room was perfect as it used to be.

The bed was made. It looked cosy. Comfortable.

And even though the radio wasn't on in here, like it always used to be, if Billy concentrated enough, he swore he could still hear it playing away.

But then he came back to the present.

He came back to the present, and he saw it was empty.

He saw there was nobody here at all.

Empty bed.

Pictures of Mum and Dad on the peach-coloured walls.

Teddy bears in the far corner of the room, over on Mum's side of the bed.

But no sign of Mum or Dad.

He stepped out of Mum and Dad's bedroom, a lump in his throat, and he walked down the hallway towards his room.

He stopped. Stopped right outside.

Held his breath.

Whatever he was going to find in here... he had to be ready for it.

Even though deep down he knew exactly what he was going to find.

He pushed the door open.

He saw his little bed over at the back of the room. Saw his

computer and his Xbox. He saw his Scooby-Doo toys and his Action Men. He saw his telescope.

And seeing all these things, it made him feel warm for a moment. It made him feel comfortable for just a moment.

Then he had another thought.

A horrifying thought.

It meant nothing.

None of it mattered.

None of any of it mattered anymore.

Because this place was empty.

Nobody was home.

He really was just chasing ghosts.

He stood there and looked over at his bed when he heard the floorboards creak right beside him.

When he looked up, he saw Kayleigh staring down at him.

She didn't say anything. There was nothing she *could* say.

All Billy could do was stand here in the place he once called home, so desperately searching for a trace of comfort, family, and connection.

And as much as he tried to hold back the emotion, to stop the tears... Billy cried.

CHAPTER FIVE

Billy lay in his old bed and stared up at the luminous stars on the ceiling.

It wasn't as comfortable as he remembered it being. It was cold, too. He couldn't stop shivering. When he used to sleep here, he used to push his feet against the radiator next to his bed if he was cold at night and feel the warmth spreading right through his body. He'd keep them there so long that they started hurting, and he ended up struggling to walk the next day. But it got him out of P.E. sometimes, so he couldn't complain.

When he pressed his feet against the radiator now, he felt nothing but biting coldness. Iciness from the metal, which hadn't been switched on for so, so long.

He thought about Mum and Dad. He'd thought a lot about coming back here while he'd been away. Thought about walking through the front doors and seeing Dad standing there, smile on his face. Holding a hand out to him, scruffing his hair.

You've done good, Billy-Bob. Real good. Proven you're tough. Way tougher than I thought. My strong boy.

And just imagining these words... it made him feel good. It made him feel special. It made him feel like his dad believed in him. That's all he wanted to prove to Dad. That he was strong. That he wasn't weak like Mum always said he was.

He remembered waking one night and hearing an argument between them. Dad was saying they needed to stop giving Billy his medication because it was useless. That it was all a sham. Mum was going mad, crying, saying it kept him "healthy".

He thought Dad was just being harsh. Thought he was being tough on him. Because he needed his medicine. Of course, he needed his medicine.

But now... well. He was still here, all these years on. He was still alive. So maybe Dad hadn't been lying about that.

Maybe Mum really was a "neurotic bitch," something Billy didn't properly understand at the time.

Dad said a lot of things to Mum.

But he was his dad. And they both loved each other, and both cared about him. Everyone's parents argued. It was just how things were.

Right?

He closed his eyes even though he knew he wasn't going to sleep. Even though he felt completely exhausted. He always felt more nervous when he was exhausted. He pulled his old Spiderman quilt cover up over his face. It smelled nothing like how it used to smell. It felt damp on his skin. It didn't feel anywhere near as comfortable as it used to feel.

But it was the best he had right now.

He remembered what Kayleigh said about him chasing ghosts. About how it was dangerous or something. He didn't properly understand her when she said it. But it made sense now. Being here, being back home, without the people he was really looking for... it wasn't comfortable. It felt like a haunted house. And it just made him feel even more sad and even more lonely.

He'd been looking for something to make him feel less lonely, after everything that had happened.

And he thought he'd found that in Aoife.

And now she was gone too.

He thought of her lying there, holding his hand with her cold fingers, the strength slipping out of her. He thought about how sorry he was. How much stronger he wished he'd been.

And then he heard a floorboard creak.

He spun around, and when he saw someone standing there, he froze.

"Just me."

He sighed. Turned back away. Kayleigh.

She walked over towards his bed. "Figured you'd be struggling sleeping just as much as me. Probably worse."

He didn't say anything back to her. He didn't know what to say. He didn't know why but... he just didn't really like Kayleigh that much. He knew that sounded harsh. But he just got the feeling that she didn't really want him around. That he was a burden to her. And that she was only looking after him because of what she'd promised Aoife.

And he kind of hated that she was right about this whole trip here being pointless.

"Can I sit?"

He looked at her. Waited a few seconds. He'd rather she didn't. He really wasn't in the mood for talking right now.

But then... he supposed he couldn't be rude.

He nodded.

She sat on the edge of his bed. Stared into space. He could see her well, the moonlight shining between his curtains and through the holes eaten into them over the years.

"If you're here to go on about being right, then don't bother," Billy said.

"I... I'd love to do that. Believe me."

Here we go...

"But... but I get it. You hadn't been home since... since all this. And not knowing if the people who care about you most are even still out there or not. I get why you came back here. Not to be sentimental or anything, but yeah. It makes sense. I get why. And I'm not gonna hold that against you."

Billy swallowed a lump in his dry throat. "Well. Thanks, I guess."

She didn't seem to hear him. She just sat there, staring into space. "It's just... I don't know. I guess it doesn't matter."

"Then maybe you should try sleeping."

She heard him this time. Looked around at him. She looked sad.

And he felt bad, then. For the first time, he felt awful because he realised Kayleigh was on her own, too. She'd lost Aoife. She'd lost her friend. He was so busy feeling so bad for himself that he hadn't taken the time to consider that.

"Sorry," he said. "I just..."

"No, it's good. I like a man who tells a woman where to shove it. You're a strong kid."

He smiled a little at that. "I wish I was strong."

"You're stronger than you realise. Trust me. I've been where you are. And I guess my journey... I guess it started similar to yours right now. Going back home. Finding..."

She stopped. Didn't say another word.

He wanted to ask her about her past. He wanted to know more.

"What happened?"

She looked around at him again. As if she was waking from a dream. Then, she smiled.

"Sleep," she said. "Or at least try to. We've got a long day of figuring out what the hell we're going to do next ahead of us tomorrow."

Tomorrow. Billy didn't want to think about that or what it meant.

He hadn't found what he'd wanted to find.

Which meant tomorrow, he had to start again.

Completely from scratch.

"If you ever want to talk," Billy said, as Kayleigh stood and went to leave the room, "you can, you know?"

She stopped. Looked back at him. And for a second, just for a second, she smiled.

"You're a good kid. Bit of a dick. But alright really. Goodnight, Billy."

She walked to the bedroom door and went to step out of it.

"Goodnight," he said.

She stopped. Just for a moment. And at that moment, Billy wanted to tell her not to leave. He wanted to tell her to come here. To hug him. To keep him warm.

No. Be strong. Don't be such a weakling. Be strong...

He saw her look at him.

For a split second, he wondered if she wanted the same thing but was too afraid to ask.

And then she lowered her head and stepped out the room.

Billy was alone again.

CHAPTER SIX

It wasn't the wind that woke Billy.

But something did.

A bang. A huge bang. Really loud. So loud that he thought something must've exploded.

He lay there and stared up at the faded luminous stars on the ceiling above him. For a second, for just a second, he didn't know where he was. And then he remembered: he was home. He was at home, in bed. Of course, he was. Where else would he be?

But then... No. This wasn't home as he remembered it. This wasn't waking up in the middle of the night like he remembered it. None of this was like he remembered it.

It all came back to him, then. Coming here with Kayleigh. Searching for a trace of his family. Or just a trace of *something*. Any kind of connection would suffice, at the end of the day. Just something that reminded him of home. Of what he used to have.

Of what he couldn't admit he'd lost completely.

But he hadn't found anything here. No trace of Mum or Dad. No trace that any of them had been here for a long time. And it made him feel sad. Of course it made him feel sad. He'd be weird if it didn't.

He lay there on the mattress, which was springy and uncomfortable. Nowhere near as cosy as he remembered. He felt cold. Freezing cold. Shivery. No matter how much he held the smelly quilt covers to his face, he just couldn't warm up, just couldn't make himself comfortable.

He lay there on his back as his heart raced fast, and he thought about that bang he'd heard. Where was it? Was it outside? It must be. It wasn't in the house.

Unless it was.

Unless it was in the attic...

He felt a shiver creep up his body. He used to be scared of the attic when he was younger. Because it was so dark up there. And he felt like there were monsters up there. Lurking in the shadows. Watching him. Waiting to attack.

But now he knew they weren't real. Now he knew the real monsters were people.

And the thought that someone was up there, in his attic... that scared him even more than the monsters in the shadows.

Because he knew what real people could do.

He knew too well.

He lay there. Stiff as a statue. He could see the outline of things he used to see every single night when he was a kid and every single day when he was in this room. He could see the outline of his television right at the foot of his bed. His Xbox and his games, which were useless now.

And he could see Gus Guts sitting there at the foot of his bed. That teddy human Dad bought him. Let you pull his organs out from his mouth. Big stupid eyes staring out at him.

Granddad tutted when he bought it. Said it was obscene, whatever that meant.

But Billy kind of liked it.

He felt like Gus was watching over him, as ugly and horrible as he was.

He looked at Gus' outline right now and felt his racing heart getting a little slower when he suddenly heard a bang again.

It was outside.

Out in the back garden.

He looked at the curtains. The holes in them made him feel watched. Made him feel exposed.

He didn't want to look outside. He always found it creepy looking outside. One night, he looked out there, and he saw someone standing there, right at the back of his yard. Looked like the Grim Reaper from those spooky video games Dad played.

He'd buried himself under his covers, and he'd frozen solid. He hadn't even been able to close the curtains. He was too afraid of them seeing him that he couldn't even scream.

He just lay there, sleepless 'til the following morning.

When he got up, he found out Mrs Rawcliffe from two doors down got burgled. That someone was snooping about.

But Billy never really got over the feeling that it was a monster out there and not just some burglar.

That it was something far scarier.

He looked at those curtains right now, and he didn't want to pull them apart.

He didn't want to see what was outside.

He didn't want to look.

But that noise.

That noise he'd heard out there.

He knew he had to check.

He knew he couldn't just leave it.

He knew he had to see.

He gritted his teeth.

You're strong, remember? You're not weak anymore. You're strong.

He wasn't sure he believed himself.

But he moved forward with a deep breath.

Grabbed the curtains.

You're strong...
And then he pulled the curtains apart.
Billy saw something outside.
And when he saw what it was... everything changed.

CHAPTER SEVEN

When Billy looked outside his window, everything changed, all over again.

Outside, he saw his back yard enshrouded in darkness. The big, tall trees behind his house surrounding a school playing field. He used to be scared of those trees, too. Used to imagine beasts in there, watching and waiting to jump down and hunt him.

But right now, he didn't see anything other than what was in his back yard.

The moonlight was bright. It shone down and illuminated his yard in a blue tone. He'd heard a bang outside, but everything was silent now. Or maybe it wasn't. Maybe there were lots of noises. He didn't know. He couldn't be sure.

Because there was only one thing he could focus on.

And it was standing right there in the middle of the yard.

A person.

A person stood there, staring up at him. Looked much like the burglar all those years ago.

Only...

No.

It wasn't the same person as all those years ago.

Because standing right here was a woman.

She looked really spooky. Sent shivers up Billy's spine. Just seeing her standing there and looking right up at the window and right at him.

He thought she might be a ghost. She *looked* like a ghost. Because she was thin. Really thin. Wearing this weird dressing gown, all fluffy and white.

You need to stop chasing ghosts...

And it seemed weird, seeing her standing there in a dressing gown. Like nothing had happened. Like there hadn't been any blackout at all. Like standing here was the most normal thing in the world.

Her hair was grey. A horrible shade of grey that looked ghostly, too.

And just seeing her standing here and staring up at him made Billy feel afraid. Made him want to throw the covers back over himself and hide.

But there was something about this woman.

Something he didn't want to admit.

Something he wasn't sure about.

Something he wondered if he was wrong about.

But something he couldn't shake.

And that something?

No. He couldn't think like that.

He had to go himself and find out.

He jumped out of bed. Walked across the creaky floorboards through the darkness of his room. He never used to like getting up in the night. Never used to like walking in the darkness. Always liked a nightlight to lead his way.

But right now, he felt stronger. He felt like he didn't care what was in the room or what was under his bed, or what was lurking in his wardrobe. He didn't care about any of it.

Just that woman outside.

He reached the bedroom door. Opened it. Stepped out onto the landing.

And then he froze.

There was something there on the landing.

Something staring up at him.

A beast.

A monster.

He felt his heart racing harder and harder when suddenly he realised exactly who it was.

"Rex," he whispered. "You gave me a fright."

Rex wandered over to him, wagging his tail. Billy ruffled his fur. Would love to stay here, to give him attention. But he didn't have much time for that.

"Come on," Billy said. "I've—I've got to go somewhere. Let me pass."

But Rex wasn't budging.

He wasn't moving out of the way.

It was like he was trying to stop Billy.

Like he was protecting him from something.

Stop chasing ghosts...

He pushed Rex aside and walked over to the top of the stairs when he saw the bedroom to his right. Mum and Dad's old room. Kayleigh was in there. He didn't want to attract her attention. This was his to explore. And he had to act fast. If he held back or asked Kayleigh for help, it might delay him; might slow him down.

He took a deep breath and started to climb down the stairs when he heard something else outside.

Another bang.

Footsteps.

His instinct was to stop. Because he was scared. He was afraid.

But then, on the other hand...

Why should he be afraid?

If he'd seen what he thought he'd seen—*who* he thought he'd seen—then why did he have to be afraid at all?

He carried on climbing down the stairs, heart racing, body shaking. Got to the bottom of the stairs. Got to the kitchen door.

And then he stopped.

He could see her out there.

See her, right at the bottom of the yard.

He was closer to her now. But the moonlight had eased; the clouds had suffocated it somewhat.

But he could still see her, and something told him he was right.

Something told him it was *her*.

He heard shuffling upstairs.

Movement.

Kayleigh?

Or someone else?

He couldn't be sure. He didn't know.

He just knew he had to keep looking.

He ran over to the kitchen door. Almost slipped, almost tripped, almost fell to the floor.

But he kept on running.

Kept on running until he got to the back door.

Tried to open it, but it was locked.

"Shit," he said.

He turned around to the cupboard under the stairs where Mum always used to keep the keys, and he froze.

He used to hate going under there. Especially at night.

That was where the downstairs monster lived.

The worst one of all.

The one he never liked being alone in the house with.

He remembered Dad shouting at him. Holding him to that cupboard and screaming at him that there was nothing in there. That it was empty.

And when he didn't believe him, he threw him in there and tied the handles, and he started crying and screaming to get out.

But it was only when he stopped crying and screaming that Dad let him out.

"See?" he said, with a smirk on his face. "There's nothing to be afraid of. There's never anything to be afraid of."

He stood opposite that cupboard under the stairs, and he knew he had to conquer his fears.

And he had to conquer them fast.

He walked over to the cupboard doors.

Opened them up.

Saw the key sitting there on a hook on the back wall.

He grabbed it with his shaking hand.

And he ran out of there as quickly as he could.

Ran to the back door, went to stick the key in the lock, dropped it.

"Shit!"

He reached down and picked it up. Tried again.

Put it in the lock.

Turned it.

And then he held his breath, and he opened the back door.

He stood there and stared out at the yard. Stared at the moonlit concrete. At the deflated football Dad used to insist on them kicking to one another at the back, by the wall. At the shed, all green and mossy now.

He stood there and looked around, and his stomach sank.

Because she was gone.

The woman was gone.

He went to take a step into the yard when he felt a hand against his shoulder.

CHAPTER EIGHT

Billy felt the hand against his shoulder, and he almost screamed.

"What the hell you doing?"

He heard that familiar voice, and he relaxed immediately. Kayleigh. Just Kayleigh. He hadn't heard her coming. Didn't appreciate her sneaking up on him like that. Especially not when he'd seen what he'd seen out here.

Who he'd seen out here.

He ignored her, walked further into his back yard. It was dark, but the moonlight was bright. The silhouettes of the shed and the fences that Dad took forever installing that summer—getting more and more pissed off as he worked—didn't feel as scary now Kayleigh was here. Now he wasn't on his own.

But Billy's fear was replaced with something else.

He was worried he'd lost her.

He walked through the yard, fists tensed. He felt shivery and shaky. The wind was strong and felt wintry. There was a smell in the air. A weird smell of smoke. Something burning in the distance, far away.

Everything was so silent. There was no birdsong. Nothing at

all. The only sound was Billy's footsteps as he walked across that yard. The only sound was his heartbeat racing. His mouth was dry. He tasted vomit right at the back of his throat.

Where was she?

Where had she gone?

"Billy, what the hell's going on?"

"I need to find her," he said.

"You're not making any sense, lad. What you talking about?"

But Billy didn't say anything. He couldn't get bogged down in conversation. He had to keep looking. Had to keep searching.

He walked over to the shed. Stopped right in front of it. Maybe she'd walked in there. Maybe she'd hid inside. Or maybe she was behind it, waiting for him.

Or maybe she wasn't who he thought she was.

Maybe she was someone completely different.

But no.

He knew what he'd seen.

He knew exactly *who* he'd seen.

He heard Kayleigh's footsteps getting closer. He could hear Rex milling around too, sniffing at the sides of the garden, at the fences, cocking his leg up, and having a wee.

And as he stood there, he just listened out for any more sounds. For a bang. For a voice. For anything that gave a clue as to where she'd gone.

But he didn't hear anything.

He stood outside the shed, and he knew he was going to have to check in there. He'd have to be careful. Because if they didn't know who he was...

No. He didn't want to think about that.

They *did* know who he was.

He'd be okay.

He had to be okay.

He swallowed a lump in his throat and reached for the shed door.

"Don't think you'll have much luck there, lad. It's locked."

Billy noticed the lock, and his stomach sank again.

It was padlocked. So there was no way she'd gone in there.

The shed was off the table.

Which meant she either had to be behind the shed or somewhere else.

He walked around the side of the shed, slowly. He had images of finding her behind it. Or of her not recognising him and jumping out at him, and...

No.

He was going to find her.

He was going to find her, and everything was going to be okay.

He reached the back of the shed, and he stopped. Kayleigh was still waffling on, but he wasn't listening to her. Not anymore.

He reached the back of the shed. Tensed his fists. Stopped.

Closed his burning eyes. Took a deep breath.

He'd seen her.

He'd seen her, and everything was building to this moment.

She had to be here.

There was nowhere else she could be.

She had to be here.

He stepped around the back of the shed.

His stomach sank.

There was nobody there.

Nothing but darkness.

He stood there. Stared at the darkness. He wanted to believe she was there. Wanted to believe he could see her there. Wanted to believe exactly what he'd seen.

But how could he when there was nobody there?

How could he when there was no trace of her at all?

"Billy?" Kayleigh said. "What is it?"

He was about to tell her when he heard it.

Rustling, over the fence at the back of the garden.

Footsteps.

He turned around and looked over at the trees.

Those big trees behind the house.

There was someone in there.

He stared at those trees, and he knew he couldn't hold back. He knew he had to keep going.

He had to follow her.

He couldn't leave her.

He ran towards the back of the yard.

"Billy!"

He climbed the fence. Climbed over the top of it. Clambered over, dropped to the muddy ground at the other side.

"Billy!" Kayleigh called.

But he wasn't listening. He couldn't.

He reached the trees behind the house. Went to climb the next fence; the metal fence, which was tall, hard to get hold of, and to clamber over.

He climbed up half of it.

You can do this. You can—

And then he slipped off and fell back against the ground.

Slammed against the muddy earth with a splat.

"Billy," Kayleigh said. Beside him now. Panting for breath. Rex barking in the yard behind them both. "What the hell?"

He lay on his back, and he looked over the fence before the trees. Looked into the darkness. Looked ahead at those playing fields behind the school.

He didn't see a soul there.

Didn't see anyone at all.

Whoever was here—whoever it was, and whether it was even *her* at all—she wasn't here anymore.

She was gone.

CHAPTER NINE

"I know I'm not supposed to swear in front of a kid. But... what the fuck, Billy?"

Billy stood at the fence in front of the playing fields behind his old house. Those thick trees towered over him. Beyond those, fields. Fields where the local football team played on a Sunday morning. He used to get up and watch them. Cheer them on from his own window. His dad used to tell him they were going to go down one day, run for trials, but Billy never really fancied it. He preferred his Xbox. He preferred the comfort of his home.

He looked over there now, and he saw nothing. He saw nobody.

And that made him feel sad.

It made him feel so, so sad.

"You jump out of bed in the middle of the night. Scare me shitless. And then you come out here acting all crazy. What is it? What's happening?"

He stood there, and he didn't know what to say. He felt sick. He felt dizzy. He felt exhausted.

But at the same time... he felt excitement. Excitement

tingling, right in the middle of his chest, right through his body.

Because of what he'd seen.

Because of *who* he'd seen.

He was sure of it. Absolutely sure of it. Even though he couldn't see her clearly, and even though she looked different... he was certain.

It was her.

And that sparked two emotions. Hope, because of what he'd seen—because of who he'd seen.

And a sense of loss, too. A sense of defeat.

Because she wasn't here anymore.

She was gone now.

"Are you going to speak to me, or are you going to keep blanking me like this?"

He walked up to the fence, looked up to the top. Remembered when he was playing back here with Wayne one day. Wayne was always one for climbing things. Trees, fences—didn't matter what it was. If it was vertical, and it was bloody scary, Wayne would climb it.

And Dad always watched them both. He always applauded Wayne. He always looked at Wayne like he was proud of him.

And even though he never said it, even though he never admitted it... Billy knew Dad was looking on at Wayne with envy.

I wish you were as strong as Wayne.

I wish you were as brave as Wayne.

I wish you weren't my son...

He heard his dad's voice in his head, and he pushed his words away. He'd never said those things. And he never *would* have said those things. Dad loved him. He might not like him as much as Wayne's dad liked him, and Billy might not like sporty things like other kids. But he was still his son. And Dad always told him he loved him.

Often at night. When Billy woke up, and Dad didn't realise he was awake.

As he leaned over his bed, the smell of booze on his breath.

Stroking his hair.

Whispering into his ear.

Telling him everything was going to be okay.

Making Billy feel partly comfortable but also partly... scared.

Afraid.

Because Dad seemed sad.

And he didn't like Dad when he was sad.

He gritted his teeth and reached for the top of the fence. Pulled himself up, right to the top, right near those spikes.

"And now he's attempting to scale the fucking fence again," Kayleigh said. "Excuse my French."

Billy dragged himself up. His arms were shaky, and he felt so, so weak.

But he kept on pulling himself up, anyway. Kept on trying to drag himself up to the top.

Because he *wasn't* weak.

He was just as strong as Wayne.

No. He was even *stronger* than Wayne.

He could prove it to himself.

And maybe if he could prove it to himself... somehow, he could prove it to Dad, too.

He tried to pull himself up and over the fence when he lost his strength and fell again.

He lay there on his back. Aching everywhere. Mud all over him, cold and sticky. He felt like an idiot. A weak idiot. He'd made a fool of himself. A real fool of himself. He should be ashamed. Especially in front of Kayleigh, too.

"You know what you need?" Kayleigh asked, holding out a hand. "A boost over. If you're so dead set on climbing over and you aren't gonna tell me why, at least let me boost you, for Christ's sakes."

He looked at her hand, and he wanted to grab it. Wanted her to help him up.

But then he just pulled himself up to his feet himself.

Stood up.

Dusted himself down.

"I don't need a boost."

He turned to the fence again. Grabbed it, started to drag himself up.

His arms started buckling again, right in the same place.

His stomach hurt like mad. Ached like crazy.

He wanted to pull himself up and over that fence... but he just didn't know if he was strong enough.

No. You have *to be strong enough.*

He squeezed his eyes shut and clenched his jaw and tried and tried to pull himself up and over that fence...

And then he fell again.

This time, he hurt himself even more. His back ached. His head didn't feel much better. And he'd bitten his tongue, so he could taste blood.

"Billy," Kayleigh said. "That's it. That's enough. I'm starting to think you've fucking lost the plot here. So you'd better explain to me what you saw. You'd better tell me what the hell is going on. Because if you don't... well, I'm not hanging around here forever."

He lay there on the muddy ground and stared up at Kayleigh as she looked down at him, bemused expression on her face.

And even though he was in pain, even though he felt desperate... he smiled.

Because he knew who he'd seen in the back yard.

He knew exactly who he'd seen in the back yard.

And the significance of that discovery was only just beginning to dawn on him.

"Mum," he said.

"What?"

He looked right at Kayleigh, and his smile widened even more. "My mum," he said. "I saw her. I—I saw my mum."

CHAPTER TEN

"We need to talk, Billy."

Billy heard Kayleigh's words, and his stomach sank.

It was sunny. Light. Morning. He hadn't slept since last night. He was in his old living room now. Sitting in the middle of the leather sofa, where he used to always sit between Mum and Dad when they were watching telly. It was cold in here. So dusty it made him sneeze. Mum would go mad if she saw it now.

But then... she had seen it, hadn't she?

He thought back to what he'd seen. That woman in the yard. It was Mum. She looked different—older, thinner. And she looked... weird. That was for sure. She looked weird.

But it was her.

She was in the garden, and she was watching him.

So why didn't she come inside?

It didn't look like anyone had been in here in a long time. So why hadn't she just come in?

"I know what you said," Kayleigh said. "About... about seeing what you saw—"

"I know exactly what I saw."

"And I'm not gonna try and stand in your way or tell you otherwise."

"Good. Because it's like I say. I know what I saw."

Kayleigh sighed. "I just... We see things. We all see things."

Billy looked up at her. Frowned. "What are you saying?"

"I'm just... Look. You've come back home. And when you come back home, it's always going to bring back... well. Strong memories, let's say."

"If you're trying to say I imagined her, then you're wrong."

"I'm not saying you're crazy or anything like that."

"Good. Because I'm not."

"Look," she said. "I didn't see anything. I didn't hear anything. I didn't see anyone or hear anyone. But you're adamant. You have to see that from my angle, kid. You have to see how that looks. Right?"

Billy didn't want to agree with her. He couldn't.

But at the same time... he remembered how sure Aoife had been about Kayleigh and Rex, when she was imagining them.

She was certain about them. Absolutely sure they were real.

Keeping them alive in her mind for her own comfort.

But this...

This wasn't like that.

This felt different.

"I know how it sounds," Kayleigh said. "I know it sounds like I'm judging you. But that's not how it is. I'm just telling you it as it is. Telling you straight."

"Then maybe don't," he said. "Because I know what's real and what's not real. And I know I saw her."

He looked around at her. He didn't really want to see how she was looking at him, but he couldn't help it.

When he turned and saw the way she was looking at him—like he was crazy, like she felt sorry for him—he regretted looking at her at all.

"You don't believe me, do you?"

She opened her mouth. Looked like she was going to say something to try and make him feel better.

And then she just sighed again. "No. No, I don't."

Billy felt hurt. And he also felt mad, too. Because he realised just how alone he was. Kayleigh wasn't rooting for him. She wasn't looking out for his best interests. Not in the same way Aoife used to.

She didn't believe in him at all.

"I came here for you because you needed this. We all need closure. And you didn't get it. But this... this thing that you've seen. That you claim you've seen. This is different. This is a road you can't go down. You go too far down this road, and you're gonna get very hurt. It's just like I said. You've got to stop chasing ghosts, or they'll haunt the fuck out of you, boy."

He sat there in the dusty room feeling like he wanted to sneeze. His arms were sore after falling from the fence, as was his back.

He felt like crying.

But he didn't.

He just stayed strong.

He had to be strong.

That's exactly what he needed to be.

And that's what Dad would've wanted, too.

"We... we need to leave this place. And we need to keep on going. Find somewhere safer. Just keep on moving. I promised Aoife I'd look after you. And I intend to do that. I fully intend to do that."

Billy shook his head. "I won't—I won't give up on her."

"When I went home after the blackout, I found my friends dead. I found them with knife wounds in their necks. I found... I found my family slaughtered. I kept on telling myself they were still out there somehow. I kept on thinking I was seeing them. Even though I'd seen the truth with my own eyes. But... but they're gone. And there was nothing I could do to bring them back. I'm telling you to stop chasing ghosts because if you don't, it'll catch up with you. Like it almost caught up with me."

Billy looked around at her. And as much as he didn't want to leave her, as much as he didn't want to be on his own, he found himself saying something he knew he might regret.

"You should go."

Kayleigh frowned. "What?"

"I know you promised Aoife you'd look after me. But... but if you aren't gonna help me find my mum, then there's no point sticking around."

He stood up. Walked towards the kitchen.

"Where are you going?"

"I'm getting some things," he said. "Some supplies. And then I'm leaving. And I'm going to find her."

"You're going to get yourself killed."

"I don't care."

"Billy, you don't want this. You should come with me and—"

"And what?" he snapped. "Drift around? Drift around from place to place with no ending in sight? With no hope? 'Cause I can't do that. Maybe you can, but I can't. I need something. I need someone. Because I'm not..."

He was going to say it. *Because I'm not strong enough on my own.*

But he fought back against it.

Resisted it.

Pushed his dad's voice away, screaming in his ears.

"I just... I just need something more than this."

Kayleigh looked at him. That pitiful look on her face again. He saw her take a deep breath and sigh.

She opened her mouth to say something else.

But Billy didn't hear if she spoke or not.

Because behind her, at the front window, he saw something.

He saw someone.

Someone was standing right outside and staring in through the window.

Staring right at him.

CHAPTER ELEVEN

Billy saw the person staring right at him through his front window, and all the hairs on the back of his neck stood on end.

It was a woman. She had long, grey hair. And these bright blue eyes that sent shivers down his spine.

And for a moment, for just a moment, he wondered if it was her. If it was Mum. He'd seen Mum out the back; he was sure of it. He didn't care what Kayleigh said—he'd seen her, and he knew it.

But right now...

The woman turned around and disappeared out of view.

"Billy?" Kayleigh said. "What is it?"

Billy's stomach sank. Why was she running? It was just like when Mum ran away last night. Why would she run from him like this?

And now... even though he didn't think *this* woman was Mum —she looked different, older, greyer... she was running, too. Just like Mum did.

He needed to do something.

He couldn't let her go.

He had to follow her.

Whoever she was, there could be no doubts about it.

She had to have something to do with his mum.

She had to have something to do with her.

He could just feel it.

He ran around the back of the sofa towards the front door.

"Billy," Kayleigh said. "For fuck's sake, not again."

He grabbed the handle. Ran outside into the mild spring air.

The woman was nowhere to be seen.

His stomach sank to even further depths.

She'd been stood there. Right in front of the window. Right in front of the silver car in front of him. And now she was gone. She was nowhere.

And for a second, for just a split second, he wondered.

What if he *was* just imagining things?

What if he really *was* just losing his mind?

He went to look to the right when he saw movement and heard footsteps.

The woman was there.

Running across the street. Limping a little.

But it was her.

It was quite clearly the grey woman with the blue eyes.

Not Mum, but...

Whoever she was, she had to know something.

Billy ran. Ran down the garden pathway. Ran towards the road. "Wait!"

Behind, he could hear Kayleigh following. Rex barking alongside her.

And he knew he shouldn't run off from them like this. He knew it could get them in danger.

But this woman...

He couldn't let her go.

He didn't know exactly why he knew, but he did.

She was important.

"Billy!" Kayleigh called.

He ran across the street. The woman was running down between two big houses now, disappearing towards the garden around the back.

"Wait!" he shouted again. Why was she running? She was looking at him through the window, and now she was running away.

Just like Mum ran away.

It didn't make sense. None of it made sense.

He ran down the driveway. A stitch crippled him, tearing through his belly and his chest. Stupid. Stupid weak boy. He was always this way when he had to sprint. Never used to be good at P.E. in school for that reason. Always ended up "trying too hard" and getting a stitch. Trying too hard. That's what his teacher used to say. And yet he told people off when they weren't trying hard enough. Which one was it?

But right now, he felt desperate.

"Please!" he gasped. "Don't—don't run. Please!"

He ran down the driveway between the two gardens. The tall, wooden gate was locked. The woman must've jumped over it into the garden.

He shook the gate, tried to budge it, but it wasn't moving.

He looked up. Could he get up there? Climb it? It looked quite big. Too big for him.

But... fuck. He had to try.

He went to jump up when he felt something grab his back and drag him down to the ground.

He landed on his back. Banged his head a little. His ears rang, and his neck hurt.

When he looked up, he saw Kayleigh leaning over him. Hands around the scruff of his neck.

"You need to get a grip, kid."

Billy shook, kicked to get free. "Let me go—"

"You're going to get yourself killed," she said. "And you're going to get me killed, too. And you know what? I don't fancy that. I'm not fucking ready for that."

"I don't care what you want. I need to find her."

He kept on trying to wriggle free, trying to fight free of her grip. Kicking and scratching and spitting.

And she just kept on holding him down.

"You're not going anywhere," Kayleigh said. "That's non-negotiable."

He kept on trying to fight from her grip when he realised it wasn't getting him anywhere, when he realised she wasn't going to let go, and he stopped.

"Now," Kayleigh said. "Are you going to behave? Or am I gonna actually have to put you in handcuffs and walk you on a leash from now on? Not even Rex gets that treatment."

He stood up the moment she loosened her grip on him, walked over to the gate. Tried to jump up it, but he couldn't make it.

"Billy—"

"Why don't you just let me go?" he shouted.

"I know it's hard, but—"

"Why don't you just leave me alone?"

"Because I made a fucking promise to a dying friend who I loved, okay? I made... I made her a promise. And I'm not betraying her. I'm not going back on that. No matter how much we fucking dislike each other. I made a promise."

Billy looked at Kayleigh, and he noticed something. Something he'd never seen from her before

Tears in her eyes.

She looked down at the ground. Not at Billy. Her eyes wouldn't meet his, no matter what.

And he didn't know what to say. Because he felt bad. He knew Kayleigh was just looking out for him. He knew she actually did want what was best for him because she wanted the best for Aoife. She wanted to honour her promise.

"Anyway," she said, wiping her eyes. "I shouldn't lose face in front of you. Need to keep my strong face on, huh? All wearing masks at the end of the day—"

"I'm sorry," he said, his voice cracking. "It's just... I know you don't believe me, but I saw her. I saw Mum. And this woman. This—this woman. She's got something to do with it. She must have something to do with it. Right?"

Kayleigh looked up at him now. And he wasn't sure he even wanted to hear what she had to say.

In the end, he didn't *have* to hear what she said.

Because behind her, he saw them.

Movement.

Movement in the streets.

Kayleigh's eyes widened. "Billy? What's wrong?"

She looked around, and he didn't have to answer her because she saw them too.

In the streets, there were people.

People holding knives.

Surrounding Billy, Kayleigh, and Rex.

"Well, shit," Kayleigh said.

CHAPTER TWELVE

Billy saw the group surrounding him, Kayleigh and Rex, and his first thought?

They didn't look friendly at all.

There were a lot of them. Six that he could see right ahead. But he knew there were more than that. He could see movement in the windows of the terraced houses opposite. He could see more movement up the street, behind the cars.

And he couldn't help noticing the way they looked. How dirty and dishevelled they all looked. All of them wearing torn, ripped clothing.

All of them men with long beards and women with long greasy hair.

All of them holding knives.

He stood there, heart racing, feeling sick. The street was silent, so quiet. Eerily so.

Just the sound of those footsteps creeping ever closer.

"Any bright ideas now, genius?" Kayleigh asked.

Billy swallowed a lump in his throat.

He didn't want to move.

Didn't want to budge.

But he knew he was going to have to.

He knew they were both going to have to.

"Seriously," Kayleigh said. "I'd back myself in a fight. But these lot don't look like they're the kind who fight all that fair."

He looked at the woman leading the way, and he realised he recognised her.

It was the woman who'd stared through the window at him.

That grey hair.

Those blue eyes.

It was her.

She looked right at Billy. Almost as if Kayleigh and Rex weren't here at all. Like he was the only one here.

Stared right at him like she knew him.

And it made him feel weird.

It made him feel shaky. Uneasy.

It made him feel... like something wasn't quite right.

He saw the way she stood there holding her knife. Listened to Rex, growling by his side now.

And he knew they couldn't stick around here much longer.

They had to get away from here.

They had to run.

They had to...

Before Billy or Kayleigh could do anything, the blue-eyed woman whistled and nodded at her people.

And that's when they started running.

Running towards Billy.

"We really need to fucking go," Kayleigh said.

Billy didn't need telling twice.

He turned. Ran down the driveway, back towards that gate.

The footsteps behind getting closer.

"I'll jump up and lift you over," Kayleigh shouted.

"But what about Rex—"

"I'll jump up, and I'll lift you over, okay?"

He didn't have time to agree, disagree, or argue.

He just ran.

They reached the gate. Billy watched as Kayleigh climbed up and over. And he couldn't help looking back.

Looking back as that group approached.

As they ran towards the driveway.

Ran towards him.

Rex standing there, right between him and those people.

Barking. Kicking his legs back.

Hackles right up.

And that woman.

The blue-eyed woman leading the way, a narrow-eyed stare.

"Billy!" Kayleigh shouted.

He turned around. Saw her holding her hands out to lift him over.

"No time to fuck around," she said. "Now!"

He looked back again.

They were so close.

Rex standing his ground.

Barking.

"Rex," he shouted.

He didn't want to leave him.

He didn't want to let him go.

But Rex looked dead set on protecting him.

Protecting both of them.

"Billy!"

He looked back around at Kayleigh. Saw the panic in her eyes as she stretched right down for him.

"You need to grab my hands. We need… we need to go. Okay? We need to go."

He looked up at her, and he knew he had to grab her hands. He knew they had to get out of this.

But Rex…

He didn't want to leave Rex behind.

He didn't deserve that much.

He looked around once again and saw they were so close.

Two people. Two men standing right opposite Rex.

Rex standing his ground.

Barking viciously.

But neither of them were paying Rex any attention at all.

They were both just glaring at Billy with wide, hungry eyes.

Knives in hand.

"Billy," Kayleigh said. "It's time. It's now or never."

Billy stood right there and watched.

Rex's angry barks getting louder as those men approached.

That poor dog standing up to whatever fate awaited him.

And as Billy looked at him, he knew that was what strength looked like.

That was what courage looked like.

He looked at the two men approaching. Saw how dirty they were. How their thick, greying beards did nothing to cover the angry red sores all over their faces.

He looked at that woman standing at the top of the driveway. Staring on with those bright blue eyes. Watching.

And he looked back at his house across the street, and he thought of Mum.

He took a deep breath and swallowed a lump in his throat.

"Go," he said.

"Billy?" Kayleigh said.

"Just go. I have... I have to do this."

"Billy, I'm not—"

"Just go!"

He turned and looked at her. Saw her perched there on top of the brick wall beside the gate.

She shook her head. "I can't leave you. I can't leave both of you."

"And I can't leave Rex. I can't... I can't leave Mum."

She opened her mouth like she was going to say something.

And then she just shook her head.

"This isn't over," she said. "This is *far* from fucking over."

And then she dropped down to the other side of the gate.

Billy was on his own now.

He looked around at that man standing opposite him. So close to him. Serious expression on his face.

Not saying a word.

You can do this.

You're strong, Billy.

You're stronger than you think.

He walked up to him. Stepped in front of Rex.

Looked up into that man's eyes as he stood there, dead expression.

And he didn't know what to say.

He didn't know what was happening.

These people.

This group of people, all standing around him. Way more than six of them, that was for sure. More than he could count.

All so silent.

All just staring at him.

Time stood still.

He knew what he had to ask.

There was only one question on his mind.

"Mum," he said. "My... my mum. Kyla. She... she was here. I saw her. Do you know her?"

The man stared down at him, unflinching.

And that woman with the bright blue eyes just peered at him. Studied him. Like he was an alien.

"Do any of you know her?" he shouted.

But nobody responded.

His voice just echoed across the street.

He stood there with Rex by his side. Everyone so still. Nobody moving a muscle. He looked back, and he saw Kayleigh was gone. He hoped she'd run. He hoped she'd run far, far away.

Kept herself safe.

Because that was what mattered.

He was strong enough to stand up for himself.

For his family.

Even though he didn't feel like it.

He heard something, then.

Something sudden.

Movement.

The man in front looking around at the woman.

And then, for the first time, Billy heard one of them speak.

"What should we do with them?"

The woman looked at the man, and then she looked at Billy and Rex, and then back at Billy again.

She stared at him. Just for a few seconds. But a few seconds that felt like forever. It felt intense. It felt like there was some kind of familiarity there. Some kind of... connection.

And then the woman did something that sent a shiver up Billy's spine.

She whistled.

And that's when the man hurtled towards Billy.

CHAPTER THIRTEEN

The man lifted the knife and swung it at Billy, and in that moment, he was pretty much convinced his number was well and truly up.

But then he heard something.

Out of nowhere, he heard something.

A bang.

A bang from across the street.

Or was it from above?

He wasn't sure.

But it didn't take him long to realise what was happening.

The man in front of him dropped his knife.

He clutched his throat. Blood poured out, spat through his fingers as he struggled to breathe, choked for air.

Billy saw the confusion on the faces of the other people gathered around. Saw them all looking up, over to the upstairs window of the house on his right.

And then he heard more of those bangs, and these people started to run.

Someone was up there.

Someone was shooting at them.

Someone was helping him.

He watched the man fall to his knees. Watched him tumble back, even more blood pooling out of his neck, all over the grey concrete below.

He looked up and saw the rest of his people running for cover. Hiding under and behind cars.

But that woman.

The one with the bright blue eyes.

She stood right there.

Stared at him, calm as anything.

Like she was bulletproof.

Dead look in her eyes.

He looked down at the knife on the road before him. Didn't have anything on him. Ran too quickly out his front door to even think about grabbing a weapon.

So this was his chance.

He grabbed the knife.

"Come on, Rex. We'd better…"

He was about to say, "better get out of here," when that woman started pelting it towards him.

He looked at the gap at the front of the house. He could bolt across the garden. Both of them could.

But what if Rex didn't make it?

And what if whoever was firing *wasn't* his friend after all?

What if they weren't helping him but were just firing indis-criminately at everyone?

Fuck. He didn't know. Didn't have a clue.

At the end of the day, it didn't matter.

Time was running out.

He had to run.

"Now, lad. Now!"

He grabbed Rex by his collar, and he ran.

Ran towards that gap between the side of the house and the woman, getting closer and closer to him.

He saw her in the corner of his eye. So close now.

Time running out.

Gunshots still raining down from above.

Come on. You can do it. You've gotta do it.

He reached the front lawn, and he felt a scratch on his arm.

The woman's hand reaching for his arm. Those long, dirty nails scratching right through his top, through to his skin.

He stumbled. Staggered to one side.

But kept on going.

Just about slipping free of her grip.

Keep running. Keep fucking running.

He looked over his shoulder. Saw that woman lying face flat on the grass. He had a chance. A chance to bolt. A chance to get away from here.

He turned around, and his stomach sank.

There were more of those people up ahead.

Blocking the road.

So many of them. Ten of them, at least.

They had the street totally surrounded.

He stood there by the front of this house, listening to the gunshots and not knowing what he had to do, when he heard a voice above.

"Billy!"

He looked up.

Kayleigh was at the window.

She had a rifle in hand.

He didn't know where she'd got it. He didn't even register that it might be her firing.

But he looked up at her, and he knew right away that she had his back after all.

"Up ahead!" she shouted. "Down that path at the end of the terraces. The gate to the school's open. You—you've gotta go through there and you've gotta run."

She lifted the gun again, fired at someone else. Billy heard a cry of pain.

"What about you?" Billy shouted.

She looked down at him, and he swore he saw tears in her eyes again.

"I told you. I made someone I loved a promise. And this... this is a part of that promise. Now go, you stubborn little shit. You go, and you don't stop going. Now!"

Billy stood there, Rex by his side. He didn't want to go. He didn't want to run.

But when he looked around, he realised he didn't have much choice.

The woman with the blue eyes was on her feet again.

Running towards him.

Some of her people were running his way, too, clearly not as spooked by the bullets anymore.

"Go now, Billy. Go, and don't look back. And remember something. You promise me you'll remember something."

He looked up at her, tears in his eyes. "What?"

"You're far, far stronger than you ever give yourself credit for."

She lifted her rifle again. Fired a few more shots at the people closest to him.

And then he turned around and looked ahead.

Looked across the road at the path at the end of his block of terraced houses.

He looked over there, and as much as he didn't want to, as much as it filled him with sadness... he knew what he had to do.

"I'm sorry," he muttered.

And then he took a deep breath, and he ran.

He didn't stop running.

Rex didn't stop running.

He kept on running until he was through the tall metal gates and into the school grounds.

He kept on running as he looked back over his shoulder, back towards the street, to those people, and to Kayleigh, firing those bullets.

He kept on running as those bullets kept on firing.

Bang.

Bang.

Bang.

And then, silence.

CHAPTER FOURTEEN

Sheila looked out over the fields and she knew the boy had slipped through her fingers.

She thought about his eyes. The way he'd looked right at her. And how familiar he looked. She knew it was him the moment she saw him. He was just as Lucia described. Just as the pictures showed him, only older.

She prayed to Lucia. Prayed every waking moment she had, in some form or another. Prayed that Lucia would bring her luck, bring her a sign from above that better things were ahead.

The boy was way, way beyond what she expected.

And now he was gone.

She turned around and walked back, away from the field. She walked across the street over to that house—the one the woman fired at her people from.

All around, she saw reminders of that awful attack. She saw her people lying there in pools of blood. She heard gasping, screaming as they battled with the pain. She saw people sitting up against the walls in front of the houses and being looked after... and then being put down if it looked like their pain was too much to handle.

And it would be too much to handle.

It always *was* too much to handle.

But Lucia would look down on them all and give them their blessing.

And that's why they couldn't be fearful.

She walked into the house. Through the door. The smell of mould in the air. A coldness and dampness to this place. Upstairs, she could hear something. Struggling. Fighting.

But she didn't rush.

She took her time.

She climbed up the creaky steps. Reached into her pocket for her blade. The one that had served her well.

The one *he* had given her all those months ago...

I'll serve you, my love. I'll keep on serving you. As long as it takes, I'll serve you.

She reached the top of the stairs. Walked over towards the bedroom. Pushed open the door, the sound of struggling getting louder, now.

When she opened that door, she saw the woman in front of her.

She was on her knees. Her face was all bloody. She looked like she'd been in a real scrap with Sheila's people. And that didn't look like it was stopping any time soon.

Beside her, two of her people. Silent, as instructed.

She looked at this woman with the blood trickling from her nostrils, her eyes swollen, bruised and puffy, and for a moment, she felt sorry for her. Truly sorry for her.

Because she was just doing what she thought was right.

She was just fighting for what she believed was the right cause.

And who could blame her for that?

But on the other hand... she had slaughtered Sheila's people.

She had gunned them down in cold blood.

And for that, there would be consequences.

She looked at the woman as she crouched there, anger in those swollen eyes.

"What the fuck do you want?" the woman barked. "What the fuck do you people want?"

Sheila just stayed crouched there.

Stayed calm.

Kept on looking into those eyes of hers. Eyes that had seen so much. Which had experienced so, so much pain.

"I said, what the fuck do you—"

"The boy," Sheila said. "Who are you to him?"

The woman's eyes narrowed and leaked some blood in doing so. "What the fuck does that matter?"

"It matters. Who are you to him?"

The woman's eyes darted around, studied Sheila's face. Like she was trying to figure her out. "I wouldn't tell you even if you put me through absolute hell. All that matters is that he's got away. That's the only thing that matters to me. And you won't catch him. None of you will catch him. Because you're weak. And he's strong. He's way, way stronger than any of you could ever imagine."

She started laughing then. Spat a bloody blob of phlegm in Sheila's face.

She kept her cool.

Kept on looking right at that woman as she laughed hysterically.

As she laughed with a sense of defeat in her tone.

Like she'd accepted her fate.

If only she knew what fate awaited her...

Sheila waited until the woman stopped laughing. She watched as she narrowed her eyes again.

"Go on," the woman said. "Do whatever the fuck you have to do here. I don't care. I promised I'd protect that boy, and that's what I've done. I promised I'd fight for him, keep him alive, and that's what I've done. So do whatever the fuck you've got to do and be done with it."

She spat at Sheila again, right in her face.

And this time, Sheila felt a twinge of annoyance.

A rare twinge of irritation.

She wiped that blob of bloody phlegm away again. She looked back at that woman. And she smiled.

"No," Sheila said.

The woman frowned. "What?"

"I said, no."

And then she pulled out her knife—her beloved knife, the one Lucia had blessed, the one that she felt whole with, the one that was a part of her... and always would be a part of her.

And she held it to the woman's chin.

"You haven't saved him," Sheila said.

She pushed the blade into the woman's chin, cutting her skin, slicing into her flesh.

The woman shook. Tried to struggle free. "What the f—"

"You haven't saved him," Sheila said. "You have condemned him."

She pushed that blade even further in.

Even deeper into her chin.

So deep that she could feel the bone of her jaw pushing back against it.

The woman struggled even more, but Sheila's people held her in place, not budging. "What the fuck are you—"

"You have condemned him," Sheila said. "And you have condemned yourself. And you will regret it. In your final moments, you will regret it."

She saw the way the woman looked at her as she held that knife to her chin. As warm blood dripped out onto her hand.

She saw the dilation of her pupils.

Heard her breathing getting more rapid.

And Sheila knew that the woman knew now.

She knew she'd made a great mistake.

"Try to stay still," Sheila said. "And this might be more bearable for you."

She curved the knife.

Tugged back, peeling the flesh and the skin away from the bone.

"What the—what the fuck are—what the fuck are you—"

She yanked that knife back even further.

Stripped more of her skin and flesh away expertly now.

And she thought of dear Lucia.

Lucia who blessed them all.

Lucia who would favour them all in the afterlife.

Lucia who they did everything for.

Lucia... and the boy.

She smiled and took a deep breath as the blood poured right down her hand.

As the flesh and skin pulled away even more.

And she kept on smiling as the woman's struggling grew more frantic.

As her shouts grew more desperate.

And as she began to beg.

And then, she began to scream.

CHAPTER FIFTEEN

Billy heard the scream from miles away, and his entire body went cold.

It was cloudy now. Rainy. He'd been walking for some time. Just walking through this town he used to call home. He'd walked through the playing fields. He'd waited around the school for a while—not his school, another school, one that disabled kids used to go to. He'd hear them from his house sometimes. They used to scare him. Sounded harsh, but they did. The way they screamed. The way they looked at him. They always freaked him out.

But he felt sorry for them, too. Because they used to get picked on. Wayne and some of the other kids used to cycle round by Billy's just so they could go "retard-spotting". Sometimes they'd throw stones at them until Billy stood up to them one day. Told them to pack it in.

They turned around. Wayne and Jamie. Looked at Billy from head to toe.

"You say somethin', Billy?"

And he wanted to stand up for himself. He wanted to stand up for these other kids. 'Cause he felt bad for them. They didn't deserve to be treated like this. Nobody deserved to be treated like this.

But he hadn't been able to do anything about it. Because he was weak.

He'd just shook his head and looked at his feet, and they'd carried on, continued, even though he wanted to stop them, even though he wanted them to quit it.

He sat there right now under a bus shelter. It was cold here, even though, to be honest it seemed to be a bit warmer than winter. The bus shelter's windows were all smashed, except for one, which had the graffiti "Fat Cox" on it. The bus stops always used to have this name on them. Nobody knew who he was. Billy definitely didn't. He wondered where Fat Cox was now. Whether he'd made it. Whether he was still marking the bus stops with his graffiti. Whether he was even still alive.

He sat at the bus shelter. There was a bus right in front of him. An old double-decker. Posters for Eternals, one of the Marvel movies, pasted along the side of it. He'd been watching it right before the lights went out, a couple of weeks before. Although... no. He was remembering things wrong. He *wanted* to go watching it. But Dad was adamant they went watching James Bond instead.

"He needs to grow up from those comic book movies," he'd said. "Watch a proper manly film about a proper man. Maybe he'll learn a thing or two."

They'd gone watching James Bond, and he'd enjoyed it. But he couldn't help wanting to watch the latest Marvel film instead. He didn't really get why Dad banged on about James Bond being so much better than Iron Man or Black Panther, or any of those other heroes. They all were all tough as nails at the end of the day.

They were all stronger than James Bond, in his opinion. They'd definitely kick his butt in a fight.

He sat there, and he heard a whimper. Looked around and saw Rex lying with his head on his paws. Just looking at Rex made him think of Kayleigh. She'd stood up for him. She'd got into that house, and she'd found a rifle somehow, and she'd fired down at those people in the streets.

And then he'd heard those gunshots stop.

And then not long after... a scream.

He didn't know if it was her. He couldn't know for sure.

But he felt bad. Because she was trying to protect him. She was trying to help him.

And she was trying to stop him running across the road after that woman.

He'd got her killed.

He'd got her killed, and then he'd run away...

No!

He didn't know she was dead.

Maybe she'd escaped.

Maybe the scream was from someone else.

The woman with the bright blue eyes.

He just didn't know.

He closed his burning eyes. Aoife. Kayleigh. They were dead. They were dead, and he was on his own, and he wasn't strong enough. He was weak. He was weak, and he couldn't be on his own. He couldn't look after Rex on his own.

But you need to be stronger. You've got no choice. Whether you like it or not...

He thought about Mum, then.

He'd seen her. No doubt about it. He'd looked out of his bedroom window, and he'd seen her standing there, staring up at him.

He didn't know why she'd run. He didn't know what she was doing. And he didn't know why.

But it was her.

There was nothing he could do for Kayleigh now. Kayleigh was gone. He didn't know for sure, but what was he supposed to think? The gunshots stopping. Then the scream...

What could he do for her?

He couldn't do anything for her.

But he could find Mum.

And that's what he was going to do.

That's what he had to do.

He stood up, taking a deep breath. His legs were shaky, and his knees were weak.

He looked down at Rex and swallowed a lump in his throat.

"Come on," he said. "We'd better... we'd better get moving."

He started to walk when he heard something right beside him.

Something inside that abandoned old double-decker bus.

Footsteps.

And when he looked around, he saw them.

Eyes.

Watching him.

Closely.

CHAPTER SIXTEEN

Billy saw those eyes peering out at him through the murky, dusty windows of that abandoned double-decker bus, and fear completely engulfed him.

The whites of those eyes were so bright in contrast to their dark surroundings. Right there, on the top deck, at the back. Whoever it was, they were trying to keep a low profile. Trying to stay still.

Watching.

Watching very, very closely.

Billy lowered his head right away. Stared at his feet. He didn't want whoever was in there to know he'd seen them. If he ran, he'd draw attention to himself.

No.

He had to think.

He had to plan.

He had to do *something*.

But he had to be careful and cautious about it.

He stood there. Totally still. Tightened his fists. Rex by his side, ears raised, like he knew something was up but couldn't quite place what. Billy had to hope he didn't see those eyes. Had to hope he didn't draw any attention his way because right now, he needed to keep a low profile.

Think, Billy. Think.

He looked down the road. Down past the trees. Down towards the roundabout ahead. It was all so open. And the more he looked down the road, the more he wondered whether there was anywhere to go. Anywhere to hide. A few abandoned, rusty cars in the road, windows smashed and foliage taking over. Weeds all over the concrete, cracking through. Crows overhead, cawing away. Always crows.

Maybe he just walked. Maybe that was all he could do. Maybe that was his only option.

Walk, and hope whoever it was wouldn't follow him.

Walk, and hope he shook him off.

He remembered Carlton. Remembered how he'd stalked Billy for so long. How he'd hunted him down. The thought of another Carlton made him shiver.

But... no.

He was stronger than that now.

He could defend himself.

He *had* to defend himself...

Because other than Rex, he was on his own now.

He looked down the street into the distance. He had no idea where he was going. The place in Rhyl that Aoife wanted to get him to had fallen, according to Kayleigh.

And Kayleigh didn't seem to know where she wanted to go herself. Seemed happy to just drift. To just survive.

Billy wanted more than that.

Needed more than that.

But right now... he knew survival itself should take priority.

He took a few deep breaths.

Only one choice...

And then he started to walk.

He could feel those bright white eyes burning into his back as he walked down this quiet, empty road. He didn't want to look around. Didn't want to see. Because if he looked back, he was acknowledging he'd seen them.

And if that person knew he'd seen them, it might force them to act rasher. To act faster.

To hunt him down.

He gritted his teeth, which were already ground down. Always ground them in his sleep. Mum wanted him to get a bite guard, but Dad said that was ridiculous. *Nobody'll ever like him if he needs a fucking tooth-nappy at night.*

So here he was, stuck with these stumps. The grinding only got even worse over the years.

Especially when Ramiro was...

No. No need to think about that.

Not again.

He walked slowly down the road like he was wandering along a tightrope. Looked to his left and his right. To the left, some sort of old industrial site. He remembered coming here with Dad once when he'd bought him a Xbox for Christmas, and the delivery people claimed it had been delivered, even though it hadn't. Dad told Billy to go in there. Demand they hand it over. He said it'd toughen him up.

But as those blokes stood there and insisted they didn't have his Xbox, Billy slowly broke down, started crying. Ran out and begged his dad to deal with them. To help him.

Dad looked at him with total disappointment. He'd never forget that look.

He'd never forget the way he told Billy to open the boot.

He'd never forget seeing the Xbox packaging right there, staring up at him.

And he'd never forget his dad's words.

"You can have it a week later for that performance," he said.

Billy shook his head, felt a shiver down his spine. He didn't like to think about moments like that. Dad wasn't always bad. He was good. He loved him. And Billy missed him.

God, he made out like he was some kind of monster. He wasn't a monster. Nowhere near.

He looked to the right, over towards the trees. A cycle route winding between them. Tall hedges either side.

Maybe he could go down there.

Maybe he could run.

Maybe he could hide.

He found himself looking back then. Couldn't help himself. Totally instinctively.

And when he did, another shiver crept up his spine.

The person.

The one in the bus.

They were at the front window on the top deck.

Staring down at him.

He looked back at them. He couldn't tell if it was a man or a woman. Too far away. Windows were too murky.

But for a moment... for just a moment... he wondered.

What if it was Mum?

She was out here somewhere. He'd seen her. Seen her in the garden, seen her disappear.

What if it was her?

He stood there, heart racing, fists tensing. And as much as every instinct in his body screamed at him otherwise, he felt the urge to do something crazy.

To go back to that bus.

To see who that person was.

He stood there, his heart beating faster and faster, his face getting warmer, butterflies attacking his stomach.

And then he took a deep breath.

"Let's go, Rex," he said, his voice cracking. "We—we need to…"

And then he stopped.

Because he heard something else.

Footsteps.

And whistling.

CHAPTER SEVENTEEN

Billy heard the footsteps and the whistles right behind him, and he knew he was fucked.

He stared up through that double-decker bus window at those eyes peering down at him. He didn't want to turn his attention from them. He kind of felt they were like those evil angel statues in Doctor Who, the ones who moved closer to you every time you looked away. He'd found that episode so scary. Dad teased him for it. Told him it was good for him to watch things he was scared of from time to time.

But this was reality. And he didn't want to risk it. He didn't want to take his chances.

But at the same time, he could hear Rex growling at whoever was behind him.

And he could hear those whistles and those footsteps getting closer.

He knew he was going to have to check it out.

He knew he was going to have to take a look.

Please don't be who I think you are.

Please don't be the bad people...

He swallowed a lump in his throat, and he looked around.

What he saw made his legs turn to jelly.

Three people. Men.

All walking towards him, down that road.

Bearded.

Filthy.

All with knives in hand.

They looked exactly like the people he'd run away from. The ones who'd tried to capture him. The ones who'd...

No. He didn't want to think about what'd happened to Kayleigh. He didn't know. He couldn't be sure.

Even though he'd heard the gunshots stop.

Even though he'd heard that scream.

He looked at these people walking towards him down the road, and he knew he was going to have to try something.

He didn't feel safe around them.

He needed to get away from them.

He went to run across the road, towards that cycle path, when he froze.

Another man. This one had a nasty-looking dog on a leash, so strong that it was almost pulling him over. Jaws snapping away, saliva flying everywhere. Angry red eyes like a demon.

Billy stood there, and he felt himself surrounded. He felt himself cornered again. He looked down the road and knew he couldn't head that way. He looked down the cycle path and knew he couldn't head that way. He looked at the industrial site, and he saw people now. People lurking around there. People wandering around.

All closing in.

He looked back at that double-decker bus, and he knew there was only one way he could go.

He didn't see the figure standing there in the window, staring down at him. Not anymore.

But he knew they were there.

He knew they were inside.

What if it was one of these people?

Fuck. What did he do?

He heard a whistle somewhere behind.

Heard the dog barking even louder.

Rex barking back.

And he knew it was time to move.

He ran. Ran down the road. He heard the footsteps getting closer behind him. Heard them closing in on him. And he knew he had to be quicker. He knew he had to be faster than he'd ever been.

Faster than he used to be, back in those sprints at school.

None of that "you're trying too hard" bullshit.

Just had to keep on running.

He looked over his shoulder, and his stomach lurched.

They were closer than he thought they were. One of the dogs was off its leash and pounding towards him.

Focus, Billy. Focus.

He looked back ahead and saw the bus right there, right in front of him.

There was only one place he could go.

There was only one place he could hide.

He yanked open the doors to the double-decker bus. Dragged them apart and then pushed his way through the cobwebs and inside.

He went to pull them back together, and the dog appeared, right there at the door, yapping away, snapping, trying to follow him in.

Head wedged in between those sliding doors.

Billy squeezed the doors closed as hard as he could. Tried to be as strong as he could. Strained every muscle in his body trying to hold them to as the dog barked and tried to force its way inside.

Billy looked up out of the front windows of the bus. Four of those people, so close now.

They were going to be here soon.

He had to get away.

He had to be quick.

He looked down at the dog right before him. Slavering away. Evil red eyes. A lust for blood so clear on its face.

And he knew there was only one thing he could try.

Even though it was dangerous.

Even though it was suicide.

It was all he could do.

Please work. Please, please work.

He opened the doors just a little.

The dog moved closer towards him.

And then Billy booted the dog right in its face.

Just enough to knock it back.

Just enough to send it tumbling out of the bus.

He didn't have time to think.

He slammed the doors shut just as the dog jumped up at the windows, threw its full weight at the glass.

Billy backed off, even though Rex didn't look too keen. He couldn't stick around here. Neither of them could stick around here. Not with those people getting closer.

"Got to get the hell away, Rex," Billy said, staggering backwards. "Got to—got to hide."

He ran down the aisle of the bus, towards the back. It was so dusty and dirty in here. There were patches of old blood on the blue patterned seats. The floor was sticky, and cobwebs were everywhere, which made Billy shiver.

A bang.

A bang at the front of the bus.

He turned around as he ran towards the back of the bus, and he saw something.

A hole.

A hole, right in the middle of the aisle of the bus.

He had no idea how it'd got there. But as he stood over it,

staring down into the darkness of the road below, he knew it might be his only way out.

He thought about running back, about heading upstairs.

But that figure...

That figure up there...

Shit. He was going to have to try something.

Rex barked by his side.

Billy stood his ground.

Shaking.

Frozen.

Come on, Billy. Don't freeze now. Don't freeze now...

He saw those doors open.

A man stepped inside.

The dog rushed in.

It was too late for him to get to the stairs.

There was only one way he could go now.

He glanced down at that dark hole in the floor behind him, and he took a deep breath.

"Now, Rex. Now!"

He jumped down to the road beneath the bus.

Landed face flat on the road. Scratched himself on loose metal. Tasted blood.

He heard barking behind him. Felt something heavy land on him, knock the wind out of his sails. And for a second, he thought it was that dog. He thought that it was on him. He waited for the sharp teeth to dig into his flesh. For it to tear into his skin and rip him to shreds.

But then he realised it was Rex.

The fat lump that was Rex.

He lay there, face flat on the ground, and tried to move.

But he was stuck under here.

He was trapped.

He and Rex were trapped, and there was no way out.

He lay there. Held his breath. Waited for the inevitable.

Waited for the pain. Waited for the end.

Footsteps racing closer.

Barking getting closer.

He braced himself for pain when he felt something.

Something he didn't expect one bit.

Something he didn't understand.

The ground beneath him opened up, and he went tumbling down into the darkness below.

CHAPTER EIGHTEEN

Billy stared up into the darkness, and he honestly didn't understand what the hell was going on.

It was pitch black. Really smelly. Like really, really bad. It felt damp down here, in the ground, wherever he was. He could hear water running somewhere. It sounded quite soothing, in a way. Quite relaxing. Like he was sitting next to a river and listening to the water flow by nicely.

A shit-smelling river that made him want to puke. But a river all the same.

He lay there and looked up into the darkness, and he didn't get it. He didn't understand. One moment, he'd been on the road underneath that bus. Waiting for the dog and the people to grab him, yank him out, capture him, or kill him.

And now he was... well. Where *was* he? And *how* was he here?

Had they caught him?

Had they killed him?

Had he cracked completely?

He felt like he was floating down into the darkness, but he hadn't been able to react because he was totally frozen with fear.

He heard panting right beside him. Rex. So he was here too.

Wherever he was, at least he wasn't alone. Not *completely* alone, anyway.

He looked up to where he'd fallen from. His ears were ringing. But if he strained to hear, he thought he could hear something. Talking up there. And wait... was that barking?

Where the hell was he, and what was going on?

"Got some nerve," a voice said out of nowhere.

It was a deep voice. Very gruff. And it made Billy jump.

He swung around. Looked over to the left but couldn't see a thing in the darkness.

He heard shuffling. Footsteps walking towards him, cutting through that sound of flowing water.

"Coming down here, to my home. Bringin' all that fuss along with you. Got some real nerve, kid."

He stopped, right beside Billy. Billy still couldn't see him. But he could smell him. And he smelled worse than the shitty smell of this place—wherever it was.

"We should be safe down here," he said. "For a while, anyway. You're lucky. Thought about leaving you up there. 'Cause, hell. Well, who needs a kid dragging them down? Burdening um? Not me. Nope, not me."

He coughed. Spluttered. Real phlegmy cough. Didn't sound well at all.

"And a *dog*... well, I s'pose they've got plenty'o meat on their bones, hmm? This one looks particularly juicy."

"Don't touch him," Billy said.

The man laughed, then. Hysterically so. Like it was the funniest joke he'd ever heard. "Oh, don't you worry, lad. I'm just jokin'. Wouldn't eat a dog if you paid me in... well. If you paid me in whatever has any value anymore, y'know?"

Billy swallowed a lump in his dry throat. "Who—who are you?"

"Name's Steve," he said. "Not that it matters. You?"

Steve. Something seemed familiar about him. Billy felt hesitant. He didn't want to give everything about himself away. But at the same time... even though he didn't fully trust this man, he *had* saved his life.

"Billy," he said.

"Little Billy."

"Don't call me that."

"Okay. Average-sized-for-his-age-Billy. Better?"

"Maybe go with the first one."

Billy looked around. Still couldn't see anything in the pitch-black darkness. But he was starting to get an idea about this place. About what it was. And about how he'd ended up here.

"You're the man from the bus," Billy said. "Aren't you?"

"Wow," Steve said. "Nobody ever warned me I'd meet a genius."

"What—what is this place?"

"Not the sharpest, are ya? What do you think it is?"

Billy gulped again. Had to try very hard not to throw up. He'd smelled some bad smells in his time at Ramiro's. And he thought it was only because of that exposure that he wasn't throwing up right now. "I'm guessing... some kind of sewer?"

"Wow. Maybe you really are a genius after all. What gave it away? The rats everywhere? The decor down 'ere? Or the stench of shit?"

"I thought that was just you."

The man laughed again. And then that laugh descended into a painful-sounding cough. A cough that lasted slightly too long for comfort.

"Hell," he said. "I'm glad I saved yer scrawny arse, now. Didn't realise I had a bloody joker on my hands."

Billy started to shiver. It was cold. But also the shock of everything that'd happened in such a short space of time. Kayleigh. Running away from her. And then the chase in the street. And now... this. Whatever *this* was.

"I know it ain't a palace here," Steve said. "But it's like I said.

You'll be safe here. And you can stay here as long as you like. Get yerself back on yer feet. And if you haven't tried rat three-ways before, well, you're in for an absolute treat."

Billy tasted hot sick in his mouth. Tried not to throw up out of politeness.

"Got a fire goin' round the corner. You should get yourself warm there a while. Rest up. Take as long as you need—"

"I can't rest," Billy said. "I need to... I need to get out of here."

Steve was silent for a few seconds. "Huh?"

"I need to go. How do I get out? Up a ladder or any other way?"

"You—you can't just walk away, lad."

"I can. I have to. My mum... she's out there. I can't just leave her. I can't waste any time. I've got to find her. Where do I go?"

Again, Steve was silent. He didn't say anything for a few seconds.

"It ain't safe up there—"

"I don't care if it's not safe," Billy snapped. "I can't—I can't abandon Mum. I can't leave her. I need to get to her. I need to find her. I—"

"Your mum's long gone, Billy."

Billy froze. The way he said those words.

It was like he knew who he was.

He'd told him his name. But the familiarity with which he spoke...

"What did you say?"

"I said it's—it's dangerous out there. You can't go walking out there right now. Not until the loons have cleared off at least, anyway."

"Not that. About my mum. You said... you said she's long gone. What did you mean by that?"

"Oh, I just meant she's probably... Well, I don't wanna alarm you, kid. But in case you haven't noticed, we've been living in a really shitty world these last few years. And in a shitty world, shitty things happen. Usually to good people."

"You didn't say that," Billy said. "You said... you said she's long gone. Why would you say that?"

Steve started to say something. Then he sighed. "Really don't recognise me, do ya?"

Didn't recognise him? What was he talking about? Billy frowned. "It's—it's pretty hard in the dark."

"Come over to the fire. See if that jogs your memory a little. And when you do... well. Decide whether you wanna go racing outside again."

Billy felt trapped. On the one hand, he wanted to walk away. On the other... this man. Steve.

He knew something about Mum.

And he seemed to suggest he knew who Billy was, too.

Who was he?

"Come to the fire. Get yourself warm. Get some water down your neck and some rat in yer belly. Then we'll talk."

He felt torn. Torn in two directions.

Heard barking above.

Heard voices, faintly, somewhere.

He took a deep breath of that rancid air, and he realised he didn't really have a choice at all.

He nodded.

"Is that a yes?"

"I nodded."

"Like you said, lad. It's pitch black down here. And my eyes might be better than yours, might be more used to the darkness than yours. But they still ain't superhero vision. Come on. Follow my footsteps. And watch you don't fall in the water. You really, really don't wanna go doing that. If you think it smells bad now, just wait until you get that shit in your nostrils."

Gross.

Billy followed Steve's footsteps. Followed them right down

this slippery, slimy pathway. A few times, he felt himself on the edge of the path. Came close to tumbling into the water beside him.

But he just kept his focus ahead.

Kept his attention on Steve's footsteps.

He had no idea how long he was walking. And he started to wonder if Steve might just be insane after all.

But eventually, they reached a corner.

And when he turned the corner, he saw a light.

A fire. A little fire in a barrel, right up ahead.

Steve walked up to it. Rubbed his hands. His face was still covered. Still hard to make him out.

Just those bright eyes reflecting the light.

Eyes that were starting to look... familiar.

"Come on," Steve said. "I don't bite. You've seen fire before, right?"

Billy gritted his teeth and followed slowly. Stayed close to Rex's side.

And held on to his knife.

He had to be ready.

He had to be prepared.

For anything.

He reached the fire pit and stopped there, just in front of it, as Steve stoked it. And then he placed something over it. A rat. It'd been skinned. It looked anything but appealing with its long, stringy tail.

But it was food, by the looks of things.

Grim.

But hell. He'd eaten worse.

He smelled that meat cooking in the air and mixed with the stench of shit... it made him want to hurl even more.

Billy stood by the fire, feeling its warmth, and looked up at the man. His face was still mostly hidden by the darkness. But he could make more out of him now.

That thick black beard, interspersed with strings of grey.

That long dark hair, curly.

That big nose.

But... wait.

Something familiar about him.

"Who are you?" Billy asked.

The man smiled. He had a bunch of teeth missing. And the rest of them weren't in a great state, blackened and decaying. "Hello, Billy-bob. Remember me now?"

It took Billy a second to register.

But when he remembered who it was, when he realised who it was... he couldn't say a word.

Because he knew who this was.

He knew *exactly* who this was.

CHAPTER NINETEEN

"Hello, Billy-bob. Remember me now?"

Seeing this man brought it all back. He wasn't sure how he hadn't already realised it was him. He used to see him every day of his life.

But he looked... different now. He didn't have a beard before. And he used to have short hair. He definitely didn't have any teeth missing, either.

He used to look... well, normal.

"Steve," Billy said. "Neighbour Steve."

"Yeah," Steve said. "Jackpot. 'Neighbour Steve'. Although I'm sure your old pa had a far nicer nickname for me, hmm?"

Billy remembered what Dad used to call their neighbour from three doors down. *Strange Steve.* Dad never liked him, and Billy never really knew why. Dad always said he was weird. Said he wasn't to be trusted, especially around kids. Mum always told Dad not to be mean and that he was okay. And Dad *especially* didn't like that. Told Billy never to speak to him. Just to ignore him. But he always found it hard, so whenever Steve said hello to him, he'd always smile and nod back.

Billy used to feel sorry for him. He didn't really know why exactly. Just that he always seemed to be on his own. Didn't have a wife. Didn't have any kids. Didn't seem to have anyone.

And Billy felt bad for him for that. Maybe that's why Dad found him weird. Maybe it's because he was just a bit... well, different.

But Billy never really minded him. He always quite liked him. He wanted to know what he had inside his house. Steve always told him about his pet lizards, snakes, and spiders. And as much as they scared Billy... he kind of wanted to go in and see them.

He'd got a new tarantula once. Billy was walking past on his way back from school, and Steve asked if he wanted to go in and see it. Billy looked down towards his house. Saw Dad's car out front. He knew he had to be careful. If Dad saw him anywhere *near* Steve's, he'd go mad.

But a quick look. What harm could a quick look do?

He got as close as the front door when he heard Dad's shout.

"Billy."

He stopped right away. Froze. Turned around and saw Dad standing there.

A look of anger on his red face.

Like he hated him.

Not Steve, but *him*.

"Go on, kid," Steve said, chuckling. "Listen to your dad. Maybe another time."

He wanted so much to go back to that moment and stand up to his dad. To tell him no. He was going into Steve's place. He was looking at his tarantula.

He wanted to change so many things in his past and be stronger.

Maybe Dad would've even respected him more if he'd stood up to him.

He'd gone back home fully expecting to be told off by Dad.

He *seemed* mad. But he didn't say anything about it. In fact, he even bought him an ice cream when the van came. Spent a little longer on the Xbox with him than normal.

And Billy kept wondering whether there was a catch. Whether he was teaching him a lesson. Whether he was going to turn on him instantly, and it was all building up to something. Maybe he was going to spike his ice cream. Maybe he was going to smash his Xbox. He couldn't enjoy any of it for that reason.

And maybe that was it. Maybe that's all there was to it.

Maybe the threat of his dad losing his temper was enough of a punishment in itself.

"How... how long have you been down here?" Billy asked.

Steve smiled, rubbing his hands together in the glow of the burning barrel. Billy could see more of the sewer now. Not much, but enough. The river of horrible smelling water working its way through the sewer beside them. The movement in the corners of his eyes. Rats.

And Steve himself.

He looked thin. He was always quite a good-looking man, Mum said, something which Dad hated even more. But now, he looked completely different, with that massive beard swallowing up his entire face. Cuts and bruises and sores all over his skin. His cheekbones poked out like a skeleton inside was trying to burst from within.

But he kept on smiling at Billy.

"Oh, who knows?" he said. "Days? Weeks? Months? Years? Doesn't really matter, does it? What matters is... I'm here now. And so are you. How the hell you keeping, boyo? Never had you down as making it this far."

Billy nodded. Another person who thought he was weak, then. Who didn't think he was strong enough to survive this world.

"I mean, don't take that personally," Steve said, as if reading his mind. "I always knew you were a tough cookie. But I just mean... well. The odds of any good'uns still being here are pretty slim, huh?"

Tough cookie. He was just saying that to be kind. He definitely wouldn't think that. Not about Billy.

"Why the sewers?"

Steve puffed out his lips and chuckled, as if it were obvious. "Because no one in their right fuckin' mind comes down here."

Billy wanted to argue with him. Wanted to point out some fallacy in his logic.

But the truth?

Steve kind of had a point.

"See you got yourself a pal, anyway," Steve said, nodding at Rex.

Billy looked around at Rex. Saw him lying there, head on his paws, warming up in the heat of the flames. And then the sudden weight of responsibility pressed down on his shoulders. He was alone. He was alone, and he had to look after Rex. Kayleigh was gone. Aoife was gone. Everyone was gone.

But... Mum.

"You said Mum was long gone. What did you mean by that?"

Steve looked away, sighed. "I was just... It's like I said. Not many of the good'uns are left. So I imagine yer dad's still thriving."

"What do you mean by that?"

Steve smiled at him. Then he shook his head. "Look. I... I dunno about yer mum. But I do know she was at home for a bit. At home, then went off with a group. Army, I think. Looked decent. Had plenty of supplies. Probably lived happily ever after. And probably best you believe that."

"Why didn't you go?"

"Me?" Steve said, lifting the cooked rat from the spit, tearing some of its juicy flesh away. The fat ran down his fingers, which he licked at, before offering Billy a piece. "I mean, I had my animals to look after. As long as I could, anyway. Rat?"

He held out the rat with those big, dirty fingers, which were covered in grease.

Billy felt a little sick, a little dizzy. "I'm okay."

"You should eat."

The smells, the sight of that rat's screaming head burned to a crisp... all of it made Billy dizzier and dizzier.

"I'm okay," he said. "Really."

Steve shrugged, then stuffed his face with the rat, sucking those dirty fingers in the process, chewing those long, filthy nails. "Well, suit yourself. But seriously. You're gonna have to eat at some point."

Billy stood there by the fire. His legs were sore. His feet weren't much better. He didn't know what to do. What to say. He didn't know what'd happened to Kayleigh. Sure, he'd heard her scream, but...

He couldn't accept she was dead.

He had to know for certain. He couldn't just walk away from her. Couldn't just leave her behind.

And... Mum, too. He couldn't get away from it. Didn't care what Steve said. Didn't care how dangerous it was to go back.

He'd seen her. He knew he'd seen her.

And he couldn't leave her out there, alone.

Especially not around that blue-eyed woman and those creepy people.

"I should... I should go," Billy said.

Steve sighed. Some juice from the rat dribbled down his chin. All his charm seemed to have been sucked away in these years of solitude. "Still hung up on that whole seeing your mam thing, hmm?"

Billy nodded. Turned around. "I need... I need to know. If she's out there... if there's a chance she's out there... then I have to go. I have to find her."

Steve sighed again. "At least rest."

"I don't have time to—"

"There's some nasty folk above ground right now. If they see you, they'll kill you. Once they've done all the world's worst nasties to you. You really wanna go wandering into the belly of the beast like that?"

"I've been to hell already," Billy said. "It's nothing new."

Steve sighed again. "An hour. I don't say that for my sake or owt. I don't say that to delay you. I say that because if you ain't careful, you'll go wandering right into that path. One hour. Rest. Nap. Do whatever you want. But an hour. I'll count. I've got awfully good at counting, all on my own down here. Not a whole lot else to do, huh? But hey. All on my own is how it's always been."

Billy felt a twinge of sympathy for Steve again. He felt sorry for him. He seemed lonely. And yet he couldn't get caught up in sentimentality right now. He couldn't let that stop him with what he wanted to achieve.

But at the same time...

An hour.

What harm could an hour do?

"Okay," Billy said, nodding. "An hour."

Steve smiled. Laughed that long, awkward laugh again, which descended into a cough. "Crackin'. Just crackin'. You get yourself a seat. And by seat, I mean a patch of ground that isn't covered in ancient shit. All the luxuries here, hmm?"

Billy looked around at the damp ground. "I think I'll stand. Thanks."

"Suit yourself," Steve said, sitting down, his trousers squelching as he touched the concrete. "It's good to see you, kid. I like my alone time. But it... it's good to see you."

Billy swallowed a lump in his throat. He felt like he was at Steve's front door again. Wanting to go inside but not wanting to upset Dad.

But right now, he took a deep breath, and he took that step.

"You too," Billy said. "It's good to see you too."

He walked over to the fire and warmed his freezing cold, sore fingers.

One hour.

Just one hour.

What harm could that do?

Billy was about to find out.

CHAPTER TWENTY

Sheila looked over at the double-decker bus standing there in the middle of this abandoned road, and she couldn't understand how somebody could just disappear into thin air like that.

It was stuffy. Warm for this time of year. Clouds had swallowed up and suffocated the sun. And it made her feel even more anxious. Even more agitated.

Keep it together, Sheila.

Keep your cool.

You never, ever lose your cool.

She stood there and looked over at the double-decker bus. She'd tracked the boy, Billy, and that mutt of his right here. They'd followed him. Watched him closely. Waited for a perfect moment to launch their assault. To attack.

But then something had happened. Something had gone wrong.

The boy and the dog ran.

They ran into that bus.

Ran in there, and for a moment, Sheila thought all her dreams had arrived at once.

Because the boy was cornered in the bus.

He was trapped in there, and he had nowhere to hide.

Her people ran after him. Took one of the dogs with them. They opened those doors, and they ran inside, and that should have been it. That should have been the moment she and her people had waited for, for so, so long.

And then...

Well. She couldn't explain what happened next.

Because her people stepped out of that bus.

They stepped out of that bus, and they didn't have something with them.

Some*one* with them.

Billy.

She walked up to them, tensing her jaw, trying to maintain her composure, keep her cool. She studied their faces hard. Saw the way they looked at the road. The ways their eyes desperately tried not to look into hers. Scared little bitches. Terrified little fucks...

No, Sheila. Keep it cool. Don't let the darkness out.

She waited before saying anything to them. Before speaking.

And then finally, when she was sure she could handle whatever they said in response, she opened her mouth: "How?"

The man on the left, Carl, looked up at her and spoke first. He always spoke first. "We don't know."

Sheila felt her anger building up. Failure. A complete fucking failure. How could they lose him? How could a boy just disappear into thin air?

She took a deep breath. Tried to maintain her composure, keep her cool. "But it's a bus. How can anyone disappear from a bus?"

Carl glanced over at Mick now. Both of them looked worried.

"Speak to me," Sheila said.

"There's a hole."

"What?"

"Underneath the bus. There's... there's a hole. He must've got through there. Run away from the bus, somehow. Without us seeing."

Sheila's face grew hotter and hotter. She gritted her teeth so hard she thought they might crack. Had to take deep breaths in to stop herself exploding. She didn't like showing her temper. "How did you allow that to happen?"

Carl looked at the road again. He looked ashamed. Truly ashamed. "We—we really don't know how it happened. Not even —not even Dog knows where they went."

Sheila looked over at Dog, who sat there, wagging his tail, tongue dangling out.

She thought about ripping that tongue right out. Wrapping it around the stupid mutt's neck and strangling him with it. See how much he wagged his stupid fucking little tail then.

But then she took another deep breath.

Turned her attention back to Carl. "I didn't see him. I didn't see his dog. So that can only mean one thing. Either he's still on that bus. Or he's somewhere else."

The two men looked at Sheila with these clueless expressions on their faces. A look of utter cluelessness. Cluelessness always annoyed Sheila. It always irritated her. Complacency was something she'd tried her best to ween out of her people.

So to see it here, so glaring, so jarring, was so, so frustrating.

"You know what I'm saying, don't you?" Sheila said.

Carl glanced at Mick and Mick back at him. Both of them standing there, so clueless, so inept.

"Fuck it," Sheila said. A rare crack in her composure. She barged past them, charging towards that bus. "I might as well do everything myself around here. But I'll make sure Lucia hears about this."

She walked on, up the road, towards those double doors of the bus.

She pulled out her knife.

Just to be sure.

She couldn't be complacent.

She opened the doors and stepped inside.

It was damp and cool in here compared to outside. Dusty. A smell of rot. Of decay. Everything so dark and grimy.

She stood there on this creaky metal floor and listened for some kind of sound. Listened for any signs of life in here.

But there was nothing.

Nothing but silence.

She walked slowly down the aisle. Gripped her knife tight. She could see that hole at the back of the bus, the one in the bus floor. The boy had to be down there. His dog had to be down there. They just had to be.

Because she hadn't seen anyone run away from under this bus.

She knew because she was watching closely.

Very closely.

She walked further down that aisle, looking from side to side, methodically, slowly. Looking at every single seat. An old phone sat on one of them, long ago abandoned, worthless in this world. A pack of condoms on another, one of them open, curled up, and brown.

And as she walked on, she felt a momentary twinge of fear.

What if she'd lost him?

What if, after everything, she'd lost him?

She shook her head.

Swallowed a lump in her throat.

She didn't want to think that way.

She didn't want to let Dear Lucia down.

She walked over to that hole in the bus floor. Stood right over it. Braced herself for whatever was down there.

And then she looked over the edge.

When she looked over it, her stomach sank even more.

Darkness.

Total darkness.

And in that darkness, nothing at all.

There was nobody down there.

No sign of life.

It was empty.

The boy and the dog were gone.

Her heart raced faster. Her chest tightened.

Those bastards. Those incompetent bastards had lost Billy.

They'd lost him, and this was on them.

She thought about the damned dog. How useless it was.

She thought about the example she was going to make of it.

How much she was going to put it through.

She went to drag herself away from the hole when she noticed something.

Just in the corner of her eyes. Barely visible at first.

But she saw it.

And in an instant, all the weight pressing down on her shoulders lifted.

"Well," she said, chuckling to herself a little. "Would you look at that?"

She stood up. Walked over towards the bus doors. Looked out at Carl, at Mick, who still had their heads lowered.

At Dog, who was lucky to still be alive.

"You two," Sheila said. "Over here."

Carl and Mick looked at each other again, eyes widening.

"But—"

"Follow. Now."

They hesitated. Took a second.

And then they walked over. Slowly. Keeping their eyes lowered. Breathing heavier. Shaking, visibly.

Good. That fear was exactly what she needed from her people.

She watched them reach the bus door. Looked down at them. She saw them look at her knife and then up at her, and she smiled.

They could suffer in this limbo a little while longer. Incompetent bastards.

"The hole. Walk over to that hole and tell me what you see."

They looked at each other again.

Then they walked up the steps, into the bus, past Sheila.

"Go on. We don't have all day."

Sheila could tell they were scared. The way they kept looking back. The way they kept looking over their shoulders. The way they kept looking at that knife.

Good. You deserve to be nervous as fuck for your complacency.

They kept on walking until they reached the hole. Looked down it.

Sheila walked right up behind them, planted a hand on Carl's back, making him jump. "Tell me what you see down there."

The pair of them squinted down. Stared into the abyss. It was Carl who spoke first. "I—I don't—"

"What do you see? Look closely, and tell me what you see."

Carl stared. Squinted. He looked like he was straining to solve the greatest maths equation in existence. Which was a good thing. 'Cause his life depended on it.

He opened his mouth, looked on the verge of giving up when suddenly his eyes widened.

"Oh," he said.

Sheila smiled. "'Oh' indeed."

He looked up at her. Panic in his eyes. "I—I'm sorry. We didn't see—"

"It doesn't matter," Sheila said. "Just don't let me down again. Your mutt's life depends on it."

She looked down the hole.

Looked down at that manhole cover right beneath her.

She smiled.

"Time to go find our boy," she said.

CHAPTER TWENTY-ONE

When Billy opened his eyes, he was filled with a sudden surge of panic.

It was pitch black, and it was cold. He couldn't see a thing, and he didn't know where he was, only that it smelled like death here. He felt burning acid racing up his throat, into his mouth. He felt dizzy. He was going to throw up. Fuck, he was going to throw up...

He jumped to his feet, and he vomited all over the dark ground of wherever the hell he was.

"Shit," a voice said. "You coulda picked somewhere a bit shittier to do your vomming, kid."

Billy looked around and saw Steve standing there by a fire-lit barrel. Rex lay by the side of the barrel, soaking up the heat. And at that moment, it all came back to him.

Steve, his old neighbour, bringing him down here into the sewers.

Telling him about his mum and how she got taken away by some good people.

How she was "long gone."

And how Billy still didn't totally believe him.

Billy felt lousy as hell. He wiped his mouth, then stood back up. He felt so shit. When had he even sat down? He didn't know. Didn't remember. Last he remembered, he was dead set on not lying on this grim, filthy floor.

Just that he was only supposed to be having an hour.

An hour, and then out of here, and off in search of Mum.

In search of Kayleigh.

Because he was wrong to run away from her. He should've stayed and found out what'd happened to her.

One way or another, he needed to get away from this place.

"How long... how long was I asleep?"

"An hour. Maybe a little longer."

"You said you were gonna wake me after an hour."

"How the hell you expect me to keep track of time, kid?"

"You said—you said you were good at counting."

"Oh yeah. I did say that, didn't I?"

Billy felt pissed off at this guy. Maybe Dad was right about him. Maybe he was weird, and maybe he wasn't to be trusted. "I... I need to leave."

"And that's fine. I get your hastiness."

"I sense a 'but' coming..."

"Smarter than you look. Look, Billy. I... I'd be doing you and your whole family a disservice if I just let you wander outta here."

"You didn't care about my family."

"That's where you're wrong. Sure, your old pa I wasn't too keen on. But your mum... I cared about her. More than you realise."

Billy felt weird about how Steve said that. *I cared about her... more than you realise.* He seemed to drift off into thought when he said it, too. Like he wasn't fully present anymore.

He cleared his throat. Tried to distract Steve. But it didn't seem to work.

"Hey," he said.

Steve looked around at him. "Sorry. I just... Hey. I wanted to show you something."

"Is it the exit?"

Steve smirked, chuckled. "You always were a funny kid. Your mum always said you were smart. Come on."

Your mum always said you were smart. Billy found that comment weird. What did he know about what his mum thought? Billy knew Mum didn't mind Steve in the same way Dad did.

But how would Steve know so much about Mum?

"Come on," Steve called, walking up ahead, disappearing into the darkness. Billy didn't want him to get too far away. It was so dark and grimy down here. He didn't want to get lost, that was for sure. He'd never find his way out of this awful maze.

"Keep up," Steve said.

Billy looked around at Rex. He seemed pretty flummoxed by all of this, too. But not nearly as disgusted by his surroundings. Actually looked pretty chilled.

"Let's go," he said. "Don't want to get lost down here."

He followed the sound of Steve's footsteps. It was so awful down here. So cold and damp and dark. The floor was slippery. Every now and then, he lost his footing and felt like he was going to tumble into the river of old shit beside him.

But he kept on going. Trying not to breathe. Trying not to inhale all that rotten waste.

How could anyone live down here?

How long had Steve really been down here?

He walked further down this tunnel of darkness. Kept seeing movement in the corners of his eyes. He realised he didn't even feel that scared. Not scared of the monsters anymore. That had passed. Maybe he was finally strong enough. Maybe he was finally over all that.

"Almost there," he muttered. "Almost... almost there..."

He stopped talking when he hit a brick wall right in front of him.

He stopped. Blinked. He was sure Steve went this way.

But then he couldn't have. 'Cause it was a wall.

He tried to walk to the right.

Another wall blocked him.

Tried to move to the left.

Heart racing.

Body shaking.

The river of shit right beside him.

He was lost.

He was lost down here, and he was trapped and—

Footsteps.

Movement in the corners of his eyes.

All coming for him.

Monsters.

He wanted to curl into a ball and cry.

He wanted to run away.

He wanted to get away from here...

And then he felt a hand on his shoulder, and he let out a cry.

"Hey," a voice said. It was Steve. "Just me, kid. Just me."

Billy took a few deep breaths, calming himself down, but feeling dizzy with those smells, with the fear, with the panic.

"Just up ahead here," Steve said.

"This better be worth it."

"Trust me," Steve said. "I think... I think you'll find it worth it."

He followed Steve closely. Held on to his arm, which made him feel weak—but to be honest, he didn't even care right now.

He just wanted to get to where Steve was going.

He just wanted to get out of this place.

Steve walked the pair of them around a few corners until, eventually, he stopped.

"You just wait here. I'll just get this lit up."

He stepped away from Billy, who felt nervous again. He

stroked Rex's head to try and make himself feel better. "It's okay. He won't... he won't be long."

For a moment, he worried he'd abandoned him. He worried he'd walked away from him. He worried he really was weird, and he really was insane.

Maybe Dad was right.

Strange Steve.

Nobody got a name like that for no reason.

And what was he doing living down here in the sewers, anyway?

He was about to walk back when flames lit this place up.

Billy blinked a few times, his eyes adjusting to the light.

What was it? What was Steve trying to show him?

He squinted past the flickering flames when he saw something.

Something that made him freeze completely.

He stood there. Totally still. Unable to move. Unable to say a thing.

Filled with fear.

He saw what he was looking at.

He saw what he was surrounded by.

And his body went numb.

"Erm, you might wanna sit down, kid. 'Cause this is gonna take some explaining."

——————————

CHAPTER TWENTY-TWO

——————————

"Sit down, Billy. Really. I know... I know this is gonna take some time to wrap yer head around."

Billy looked up at the wall behind Steve, flickering in the light from the flames. He couldn't believe what he was looking at. Couldn't understand what he was looking at. It couldn't be real. It had to be fake, somehow. Doctored. It didn't make sense. None of it made sense.

But there was no denying what he was looking at.

On the wall of the sewer, there were photographs.

Photographs with Steve, smiling, in different locations. In some, he was on a mountain in the sun. Others, on a beach, drink in hand.

But it wasn't Steve Billy was interested in.

It was the person beside him.

"I know... I know it's gonna take a lot of wrapping your head around. But it's... I couldn't think of any other way of showing you how much I cared."

Billy couldn't think. He couldn't speak. He couldn't *anything*.

All he could do was look at that person standing beside Steve in these photographs.

That woman standing beside Steve in these photographs. Smiling. As beautiful as ever.

"Mum," Billy said.

Steve nodded. Sighed. "I suppose I have a lot of explaining to do, huh?"

Billy didn't know what to say. "I—I... Why?"

"No easy way of sayin' this, kid. But your mum and I, we were..."

"No," Billy said, shaking his head. He knew what Steve was getting at. He knew where he was going with this. And it made sense. Suddenly, it made sense.

His dad's hatred and suspicion of Steve.

Why he disliked him so much.

"I know it ain't a sweet pill to swallow, but it is what it is. Your mum and I were together. We were as good as a couple. She knew about yer dad's playing away from home. She didn't like how he treated her. How he treated you."

"This can't be possible."

"Did you ever wonder where she went when she disappeared for weeks?"

Billy remembered her kissing him on the head. Smiling. Tears in her eyes. Sadness in her voice. *I won't be long, Billy. And one day, we'll go on holiday together. Just you and me. We'll go on holiday together, and we'll get away from here. Far, far away from here.*

"Dad... Dad said she was just on holiday. With her friends. Or —or away with work."

"That's the story we told," Steve said, sighing. Rubbing his long hair. "I ain't proud of what we did or how we did it. But your dad... he was a loose canon, Bill. Your mum really didn't trust him."

"He said Mum was sick."

"*He* was the sick one. Your mum had her issues; don't get me wrong. But your dad was the sick one. The controlling one. He mighta banged on about how weak the pair of you were, but that's because he liked it that way. Didn't make it seem that way, sure. But that was exactly how he liked it. He liked the hold he had over you. He liked how in control of you he was. Because *he* was a weak man. And a weak man needs to make people feel weaker in order to feel strong himself."

Billy stood there and looked up at these photos. He was feeling more and more sick. More and more dizzy. It was all clicking together. All making sense now.

"My dad," Billy said. "Did he... did he know?"

"Never officially. But he did. Deep down, he knew alright. And he hated me for it. He hated us both for it. I swear if the world hadn't collapsed, he'd've murdered me anyway, one day."

Billy couldn't think.

He couldn't take anything else in.

All this news.

All of it, building and building and building.

It made him want to get away from here.

It made him want to run.

Because it meant everything he thought he knew was a lie.

His whole life was a lie.

He had to get away.

Billy turned around, walked into the darkness. "I need... I need to go."

"Billy?"

"I need to get away from here."

He walked into the dark. Didn't care where he was going. Didn't care about the monsters anymore. Didn't care about *anything* anymore.

"I spent years trying to find her, Billy. Years. But she's—she's gone. I know she's gone."

"I need to find her."

"You won't find her."

"I have to—"

"You won't find her 'cause she's dead, Billy."

He stopped dead in the darkness.

Turned around to face Steve again.

His face flickered in the flames. He looked sad. Tearful.

"What?"

"I didn't want to tell you," Steve said. His voice cracking with emotion. "I wanted to protect you."

"You're lying."

"I'm not lying."

"You—you have to be lying."

"I held her, Billy," Steve said. Full-on crying now. "I held her in my arms as she died. As she took her last breath and died. I buried her. I buried her, and then I came here and I—I didn't leave other than for food or water when I needed it. But this is where I am now. This is my life now. Without Kyla... this is all that's left for me."

Billy listened to these words, and he felt empty. He didn't feel the pain he expected to feel. He just felt an emptiness.

Mum was gone.

Steve wasn't lying.

She really was gone.

Whoever he'd seen in his garden might've looked like her.

But it wasn't her.

He was just seeing what he wanted to see.

She was gone.

"I... I saw her."

"That wasn't her, Billy. That was..."

"That was who?"

"It doesn't matter."

"It matters.

"It wasn't her!" Steve shouted. His voice echoed around the sewers.

And Billy wanted to keep on pushing him. Keep on pressing.

But in the end, he could only ask one question.

"Why did you lie?" Billy asked.

"I didn't want you to suffer."

"Who killed her?"

"What?"

"You said she died in your arms. Who killed her?"

Steve looked at him. Like he was holding something back from him. "Billy..."

"Who killed her?" Billy shouted.

"The people who were after you. They run this place now. I call them the Whistlers. That's how they communicate with each other at distance. Led by this nut job, Sheila. Worship some make-believe god called Lucia. Bunch of total crazies. I had... I had my share of run-ins with 'um, let's put it that way. But they're dangerous. And they're smart. Doesn't matter how nonsensical what they worship is. They've found meaning, and they're hell-bent on keeping their shitshow going."

Billy swallowed a lump in his throat. The Whistlers. Sheila. They'd killed Mum, and as far as he knew, they'd hurt or killed Kayleigh, too.

"Why do they want me?"

"It's—it's complicated. But these... these people aren't logical. Just don't let 'um get you. That's all you need to remember, really."

Billy wasn't convinced. "What about Dad?"

Steve looked at him. Frowned. "What about him?"

"You said Mum died because of the Whistlers. What about Dad?"

Steve stared at Billy for a few seconds longer than was comfortable. He opened his mouth like he was going to say something. Then he looked away. "I don't know about your dad."

"Rubbish," Billy said.

"Huh?"

"You know something. You know more than you're letting on."

"Look," Steve said. Firmer now. "I know this ain't easy for you to take in. But not everything's a conspiracy, kid. You need to stop chasing the past. Seriously. Sometimes... sometimes the past's better left buried."

You need to stop chasing ghosts...

He'd heard that before.

"These Whistlers," Billy said. "Their camp. It's near our old street?"

Steve nodded. Shrugged. "I guess so."

Billy tightened his grip on his knife. "Then that's where I'm going."

"What?" Steve said.

"If they killed her... then they are the ones who hurt Kayleigh, too. And they—they can't get away with it. I can't let them get away with it. I need to get out of here. And I need—I need to find Kayleigh. I need to know. And I need to stop them."

He walked back, out into the darkness.

"Billy, you can't just go charging up there—"

"That's more than you've ever done about them, isn't it?"

He felt bad for snapping at Steve. But he had a point, didn't he? What had Steve done to try and get to the people who'd killed his mum? Who'd killed the woman he supposedly loved?

"I... I tried fighting. But there's nothing to be gained from it."

"So you just sit down here like a rat and feel sorry for yourself?"

"Careful," Steve said.

"No," Billy said. "I'm sick of being careful. I need... I need to find them. I need to make them pay. For what they did to Mum. For what they did to Kayleigh. How do I get out of this place?"

"I'm not letting you just walk out of here."

"You're not my dad," Billy said. "Tell me. Tell me how I get out of here?"

Steve froze.

He didn't say anything for a few seconds.

And it was those few seconds that scared Billy.

That made him wonder even more.

What if...

Steve sighed. He lowered his head. "That's the thing, kiddo. Don't mean to go all Darth Vader on your ass. But... but I kind of am your dad."

Billy's mouth went dry.

He felt the ground opening beneath him.

He didn't know what to do.

What to say.

He wanted to vanish.

He wanted to disappear.

"Wh—what?"

Steve's smile widened. He went to say something else to Billy. Make some other joke. Some other wisecrack.

And that's when Billy heard it.

A bang.

A bang, somewhere in the darkness.

A bang followed by silence.

And then, whistling.

"They're here," Steve said.

CHAPTER TWENTY-THREE

Billy heard the whistles echoing in the darkness.

He squinted into the pitch-black dark towards where those whistles were coming from. He couldn't see a thing. And judging by the lack of lights heading towards him, neither could whoever was coming.

Just those echoing footsteps.

Those echoing whistles.

Getting closer and closer...

"We need to get a move on, Billy," Steve said. And it all seemed so bizarre. It all seemed so surreal. Steve had just dropped an absolute bombshell. He'd told him he was having an affair with Mum. And not only that, he'd told him he was his dad...

And Billy just felt numb. He didn't feel anything about it whatsoever. He didn't know if it was just shock or if he'd already been through so many things in his life that nothing got to him anymore. He hadn't had any time to process it.

He just knew that the people who had done whatever they'd done to Kayleigh were in the sewers now.

The people who'd killed Mum were in the sewers now.

And they were coming for them both.

"Billy," Steve said, putting a hand on his shoulder. "You listen to me. These people, you don't know 'um like I know 'um. They're savages. And if you don't follow me right now, they'll eat you for breakfast. And I mean *literally* eat you for breakfast, too. Understand?"

Billy wanted to stand his ground, as those voices and footsteps got closer. He wanted to fight against these people. Because they'd killed people close to him. And he felt angry at them. He felt so, so angry at them.

He saw himself standing over Carlton's body again.

Saw himself ramming that knife into his throat and his chest and his face, again and again and again.

He knew what it felt like getting revenge, and he wanted to go after them right now for what they'd done.

He wanted to be strong.

But at the same time...

He knew down here in the sewers, Steve was right.

"Billy, come on."

He swallowed a lump in his throat, and he turned around and followed Steve into the darkness.

He ran. Ran along with him, Rex following closely behind. He slipped a few times on this damp, mossy floor full of gunk, almost tumbling to his knees. He had no idea where he was going. And he didn't trust Steve. How could he trust him after everything he'd just been told?

But he trusted Steve knew this place better than anyone.

So right now, he needed this man on his side.

"Not much further," he said.

They ran further into the darkness. Those footsteps and those whistles sounded like they were getting further away. Billy had no idea where they were going, but he had to guess there was a hiding place up here somewhere. Or a way out of here.

"There's some ladders up ahead," Steve said. "They'll take us right up near one of them industrial units. I know some places to hide around there. We go up there, and we…"

He stopped.

Because he heard something.

Exactly what Billy heard.

Banging up ahead.

Whistling up ahead.

Footsteps up ahead.

"Fuck," Steve said. "They've—they've got in through the other side."

Billy froze. Heard those footsteps coming from both sides now. "What do we do?"

He heard Steve panting. Saw him looking around, his silhouette searching the darkness. "We—we've got no choice."

"What do you mean?"

"In the water."

"What? No fucking chance."

"Language, kid."

"Is now really the time to be having a go at me for my language?"

"It's never a bad time to be having a go at you for your language. Look. You need to hurry. We all need to hurry. Before it's too late."

"There has to be another way."

"There isn't another way."

"There has to be."

He stood there in the darkness, and he heard those footsteps getting closer and closer. And as much as he really didn't want to get into that dark, cold, horrible water, he knew he might not have a choice.

"Just cover your nostrils. And don't let any of it get in your mouth or your eyes. Preferably don't let it get anywhere. But… but believe me. It gets a bit more bearable after a short while."

He looked down into the darkness below. Like black treacle. He dreaded to think of all the disease and germs floating around in here. Years and years of shit and piss and God knows what else that hadn't been washed away. Whole new breeds of infection in here.

And yet, what was the alternative?

Wait here for the Whistlers to arrive?

He heard those whistles getting closer.

He heard them closing in.

And he knew he had no choice.

"Now," Steve said. "Now!"

Here goes nothing...

He closed his eyes, covered his nostrils, and he slipped into the water.

It was like falling into the belly of a monster.

The water wasn't like normal water. It was thick and slimy. Felt like it was creeping up his skin, eating up every inch of him.

And the smell... in here, the smell was even worse. It wasn't all liquid, either. Solids were floating around. He dreaded to think what they might be. Better not to even think about it.

He heard a splash beside him, covering him in this awful water. It splattered in his eyes and mouth. And the taste... the taste was worse than anything he'd ever tasted. Like vomit, shit, piss, and what he imagined dead bodies to taste like, all mixed together as one.

But Rex was in the water with them now. And he seemed to be enjoying floating along. Good-for-*fucking*-him.

Billy felt something on his arm. Looked around. It felt like a hand. "Did you—did you just touch me?"

"No," Steve said. His voice coming from the other side.

"I—I swear I felt a hand."

"You probably did," Steve said.

He didn't have to say anything else.

"Now come on. We're gonna have to swim a little. I know a little alcove we can hang out until..."

He stopped.

Because out of nowhere, the section of the sewer they were in lit up.

Billy turned around, and he saw them standing there, one of them holding a flame-lit torch.

"They're—they're here," Steve whispered.

CHAPTER TWENTY-FOUR

Billy floated in the filthy water and tried to keep as still and quiet as he possibly could.

The pitch-black darkness of this sewer had been lit up by that flame-lit torch of the man standing right there, on the little path at the side of the sewers. He was so close. Just a few metres away. So close Billy could swim over and touch him.

He had to stay still.

He had to hold his breath.

He had to stay as quiet as possible.

The Whistlers were here.

They were here, and they were looking for him.

Steve floated alongside Billy, staying as still as possible too. He stared up at the man standing right there at the water's edge. He couldn't look away from him. Had to make sure he watched him at all times.

And then there was Rex, too. Rex, who Billy held on to. Stroked his damp, slimy fur. He prayed he'd stay still. Prayed he'd resist his doggy instincts to go swimming off, splashing around and drawing attention to them all.

The air was thick with the stench of shit, rot, and death. The icy cold water was like gooey treacle all over Billy's skin. He could taste it in his mouth, too, like rotting flesh.

He didn't think he'd ever scrub this smell away from his body. From his skin.

He didn't think he'd ever un-smell it.

He floated there and stared at the side of the water as he saw more people emerge from the darkness. And as much as Billy wanted to say something, as much as he wanted to *do* something —because these people had killed Mum and done God knows what to Kayleigh—he knew right now there was nothing he could do but wait here.

Pray.

He watched as more of them filled this section of the sewer. They were silent. Whispering amongst one another. None of them were looking over towards the water. None of them were looking this way.

But Billy knew it would only be a matter of time.

Eventually, they would look.

Eventually, they would see him.

And then...

Well, what then?

He didn't know. He couldn't be sure.

He floated there when suddenly he felt Rex begin to wriggle and try to shake free.

He held Rex tighter. He couldn't have him kicking around in the water. Couldn't have him making a fuss. He couldn't have him drawing attention this way.

"Rex," Billy whispered. "Please. Not now. Good boy. Please."

But Rex didn't seem to be stopping.

He kicked and splashed at the water.

Billy looked up, and he saw something that filled him with total fear.

First, the dog. The one who'd chased him into the double-decker bus.

It was here. And it was sniffing around the water's edge.

And then the man holding the flame lit torch.

He was beginning to turn around.

Beginning to look this way.

Billy held his breath and gripped onto Rex because he knew what he was going to have to do.

He hated the thought of it. But he knew exactly what he was going to have to do.

The only thing he could do.

And right on cue, Steve said the word that confirmed all his worst fears.

"Down."

He didn't even have time to think about it.

He closed his eyes, pinched his nostrils, and he descended into that dark, sticky mess of sewer water below.

When he was down there, he squeezed his eyes shut. He felt things hitting his face. Solid things passing by. He clenched his lips together, but it wasn't stopping the awful taste seeping through. He held on to Rex, who struggled even more now. Poor boy. He wouldn't understand. But he had no choice.

He floated down there for as long as he could.

Running out of breath.

Getting dizzier and dizzier...

He didn't know how long he'd been down here, or how long to stay down here.

He just knew he needed to get back to the surface.

He just knew he needed to breathe.

He stayed down there as long as he possibly could until finally, he let himself float back to the surface.

And when he did, he gasped for air.

He looked up. Over at the side of the sewer water.

They'd walked on.

The bloke with the torch had walked on.

"Good. Now... now swim. To your left. Slowly."

He waded through the water alongside Steve, holding Rex, who panted away. Billy shivered, a combination of cold and adrenaline. His skin was covered in all sorts of things. Old hair was wrapped around his fingers, all slimy. Every now and then, he felt sharp things digging into his skin and pictured needles floating along with him.

"Just through that grate," Steve said. "But I hate to say it. We're gonna have to go under again."

We're gonna have to go under again.

Of course, they were. Of course, they fucking were.

Billy looked back over to the side of the sewer water. He looked at those dark figures passing by. Watched them getting fewer and fewer. They had a chance to get away from here now. It wasn't an ideal route. But it was a chance all the same.

He went to take another deep breath of that awful air and descend when he saw someone up ahead.

Another person holding a flame-lit torch.

Only...

No.

It couldn't be her.

That couldn't be possible.

And yet...

"Kayleigh?" he said.

"Billy," Steve whispered. Firmly.

Billy went to swim off towards the side of the water. Because it was Kayleigh. He'd seen her face, just like he'd seen Mum's face earlier.

It was her.

It had to be her.

And yet there was something different about her.

Something *off* about the way she was moving.

Her body was... *different*, somehow.

"Billy!" Steve gasped.

Billy bobbed towards the side of the water, towards that

person, towards Kayleigh, when suddenly he heard something that sent a shiver creep right up his spine.

Rex.

Rex was barking.

Out of nowhere, the woman who looked like Kayleigh turned around and pointed the torch towards him.

He couldn't see her face anymore. The light in his eyes was too bright.

But he could hear Rex barking away.

And he could hear something else.

Something that sent shivers right up his spine.

Whistling.

Whistling, echoing through the sewers.

Whistling, getting closer and closer and closer.

"We need to get the fuck out of here, Billy," Steve said. "We need to get the fuck out of here. Now!"

____

CHAPTER TWENTY-FIVE

____

"Billy! We need to get out of here! Now!"

Billy had found these Whistlers scary since he first saw them. They looked savage. They looked unclean. Something about them just looked... off.

But right now, hearing their whistles fill the sewers and knowing full well they were onto him, he felt even more scared than ever before.

Those whistles getting louder and louder.

Bouncing off the sewers' brick walls.

Closing in...

He floated there by the side of the path at the side of the water, and he looked up at that woman holding the torch. The one who looked like Kayleigh.

No.

The one who *was* Kayleigh.

It had to be her.

He could make out her face in the glow.

It *was* her.

"Kayleigh," he said. "What... what..."

And then he heard footsteps.

He heard more barking. The dog. Not Rex, now, but their dog.

"Billy!" Steve shouted.

Billy wanted to stay by the side of this river of shit. He wanted to know what the hell was going on. He wanted to know why Kayleigh was standing here with these people. And why she wasn't saying a word to him.

Had they kept her alive?

What had they done to her to make her like this?

How had they got to someone as strong as she was?

He looked up at those flames flickering just in front of her. Her face was mostly hidden in the darkness now, but he could still see thin strands of blonde hair trailing from her head. Her arms looked longer than he remembered. Her legs looked different, too. Wider, somehow.

He didn't know what was happening, but he knew one thing for sure.

The Whistlers were onto them both.

"Billy," Steve said, grabbing his shoulder out of nowhere. "You and your yappy mutt. Outta here. Now."

And as much as he wanted to hold back, as much as he wanted to understand what was happening here, Billy knew there was nothing else he could do here—if he wanted to live.

So he swam away with Steve. Back towards that grate. Away from the swathes of Whistlers approaching the bank of the sewer water.

"Remember what I said," Steve said. "Got to go under. Got to go quite a way, too. And then you just swim straight the fuck on. I'll tell you when we get to the exit. But in case... in case we don't make it. In case *I* don't make it. Look for the light shining down into the water. You'll know you're right by the exit then. Understand?"

Billy didn't fully understand. He couldn't take any of this in.

The light shining down into the water.

The thought of Steve not making it...

No.

That couldn't happen.

But he nodded. Because he knew he had to.

"Right." Steve patted his shoulder. Gasping for air. "Down and under. You've got this. You've *gotta* got this. Okay? Or it's over. Don't mean to mince my words… but it's over."

Billy looked at Rex. He stroked his fur. That chorus of whistles still filling up these sewers. So close now.

He looked into the darkness of Rex's brown eyes and stroked that fur even more.

"Down and under, lad," he said. "Down and under. We'll make it. You and me will…"

And then he heard something that filled him with terror.

A splash.

And then another splash.

And then another.

And another.

"They're comin'!" Steve shouted. "Down and under, Billy. They're comin'!"

He looked around, and he saw the figures swimming his way.

He saw more of them jumping into the water like it was nothing at all.

Why did they want him so badly?

What did they want with him?

"Now or never," Steve said.

And Billy knew not to mess around.

He knew Steve was right.

He wished he had more time. Because these might be his final moments with Rex.

But he couldn't afford to stick around any longer.

"Now, Rex," he said. "Now!"

And then he held his breath, and he ducked under the water.

It was so dark down here. So murky. He couldn't see a thing. There were so many horrible things floating around, too. Nasty, solid things and softer things, too. They kept hitting his face, getting in his eyes. He knew he'd probably be blind by the time he was done in here. He knew he'd probably die of whatever he'd got in his mouth and nostrils.

But he had to swim down.

He had to keep going down.

He held on to Rex's paw and went to go down, down into the darkness, down towards whatever was below.

That's when he felt it.

A hand.

A hand around his ankle, dragging him back.

He opened his mouth and screamed instinctively, which was a terrible idea because it filled his mouth with this awful water.

He tried to kick back. Tried to grab onto something for support—anything at all.

But it was too late.

Whoever it was, they were dragging him up.

They were dragging him up and—

A hand.

A hand from below.

Pulling him down.

He felt some tension.

Felt some struggling.

Then, in the darkness of the water, he swore he tasted that rusty metal tang of blood.

But that hand.

That hand around his.

Steve's hand.

He felt it, tightening around his.

Squeezing it a few times. Like he was reassuring him.

And then he started to swim again.

He kept on going down into the darkness. Already out of breath, already desperate for air in this icy water. Rex was still by his side. He felt against the rough, uneven brick wall. Felt for that opening. He was getting dizzy, running out of air. He needed to get to the bottom, and he needed to get there fast.

He kept on going, and his mouth opened. He breathed in a little water, making him want to puke. He felt Rex kicking around, too. Struggling. Like he was trying to get out of this too.

But he kept on going.

He kept on going because he had no choice.

He started to think about turning back for air when he suddenly felt an opening.

Here. We've got it, Rex.

He swam underneath it.

Swam with what little strength he had left.

And then he pulled Rex underneath it, too, with that remaining little strength.

He pulled him under.

We did it.

He looked up.

Further into the darkness.

You've got it. You've...

He swam up.

Up towards the heavens above.

He needed to breathe.

He needed to open his mouth.

He needed air.

Just keep going...

He kept on going and going.

Just a little further...

His muscles seizing up.

His heart beating faster than it'd ever beat in his life.

His legs and his feet shaking.

Breathe, Billy. Breathe.

No!

He went to climb this wall of water some more when he felt it, almost instantly.

The energy drifting from his body.

The last of his strength slipping away.

His hands seizing up.

His mouth opening.

And...

Just let a little water in, Billy. It won't do you any harm...

As much as every instinct in his brain told him not to, Billy stopped holding his breath and breathed in.

CHAPTER TWENTY-SIX

"Billy. Billy!"

Billy opened his eyes, and he gasped.

He heaved up awful tasting stuff all over the place. It burned at the back of his throat. It tasted so bad. He couldn't see anything. It was dark. Pitch black. And he was freezing cold. Shivering all over.

"That's it," the voice said. Steve, by the sound of things. "You get it all up. But we don't have long. Won't be long 'til they figure out how we got through. You hear me?"

Billy looked around and squinted. His eyes were sore and burning, probably from all the gunk he'd got in them. He could just about make Steve out, sitting beside him on... well, wherever they were. It was clear they were still in the sewers; he knew that much. Those smells and tastes hadn't gone away, even if he *knew* he'd probably smell and taste the sewers for the rest of his life, no matter how far away he was from them.

"Come on," Steve said, rubbing his back, patting it, trying to get more of that sick and water up. He must've passed out. Passed out right before he'd escaped.

Blurry memories of someone reaching in and pulling him up to the surface...

"Rex," Billy said.

"He's okay," Steve said. "Right here next to me. Not a dog person, y'know. Never been one for pets. But this mutt? Yeah, he seems loyal. He seems cool. Good little companion for you, huh?"

Billy nodded. He stroked Rex's damp fur. He felt so bad. He'd almost lost him. Rex must've been so confused when he was dragging him down, deep into the water. He must've thought he was trying to hurt him. Must be why he wasn't sitting with him now.

He bet Rex wondered where Aoife was, still. And now, where Kayleigh was. Because Billy was hardly leadership material.

But he just had to do his best. That's what mattered. Mum told him that about his hamster, Snowy. *You'll be surprised, Billy. Surprised just how capable you are.*

Looking after his hamster, caring for it... it used to give him a sense of purpose. A sense of responsibility.

He missed his hamster.

He heard whistling and banging to his left. Looked around at the dark sewer walls.

"Don't worry," Steve said. "It's like I said. We're good for now. But they're gonna come up the other side of that grate. I wanna be long gone before that happens. You hear me?"

Billy nodded again. He felt so drenched. So cold. So weak.

"Come on," Steve said. "I know movin' ain't exactly gonna be top on yer list of priorities right now. But it's summat we're gonna have to do. Like I say. Time ain't exactly a luxury for us."

Billy looked at the dark silhouette of a man, and he still couldn't believe what he'd learned about him. He still couldn't believe the things he'd told him.

He was his father.

His real father.

Dad... Dad wasn't his real dad. He was just Mum's husband.

Steve had an affair with Mum. Went on holidays with Mum.

And then Mum died in his arms.

Died because of the Whistlers.

Because of Sheila.

He listened to those footsteps. Listened to those whistles. And he thought about how much he wanted to hurt Sheila. How much he wanted to hurt them all. For the things they'd done. For the lives they'd taken.

And then he heard it.

The sound of someone emerging from the water, just up ahead.

The sound of gasping.

Steve stood up slowly.

Rex started to growl.

"Come on," Steve said, grabbing Billy's hand. "We've got to get moving. We've got to get out of here. Quick!"

He ran. Turned and ran. Turned and ran even though Billy wanted to stay here and fight them. Even though he wanted to show how strong he was.

To stand up for himself.

To look them in the eye and tell them he was the son of the woman they'd killed.

To avenge his mother.

But then, as he ran quicker down this pathway, he thought about Kayleigh.

How he'd seen her holding that torchlight.

It was her face. For just a moment, he'd seen her face.

Just like he'd seen Mum's.

It wasn't a figment of his imagination.

But it didn't add up with what Steve was saying.

"What—why did I see—"

"Not the time," Steve said. "Up ahead. Look!"

Billy looked ahead, and it took him a few seconds, but he saw it.

A beam of light shining down up ahead.

The first natural light he'd seen in God knows how long.

"Over there," Steve said. "Over by the light. Up the ladder."

Billy saw that light up ahead. It was close... but he felt exhausted. He felt like he couldn't run much further.

But he had to.

Footsteps behind.

Footsteps getting closer.

Footsteps and whistling.

"Come on," Steve said. "Almost there. We're—we're almost there."

He looked back again.

Saw those shimmering dark figures getting closer.

"Quick, Billy. Quick!"

And then he looked back ahead.

One final push.

One final fucking push.

He slammed into something.

Something that almost knocked him to his feet.

Something that he only realised at the last second was Steve.

"Here. Up the ladder. Now."

Billy shook his head. "But—but Rex—"

"Ain't no time to mess around, kid. It's up the ladder or game's up."

Wait. What? "I'm not leaving Rex behind."

"Then you're a dead kid. I'm sorry. I know he's been a good pal for you. But—but there ain't no other way. Up the ladder. There's no more time. Now."

Billy stood there, and he looked at Rex.

He saw him looking back up at him, tongue dangling from his mouth like a slice of pink ham, tail wagging behind him, ears raised. Like he was waiting for the next step in this mad adventure.

And then he heard those footsteps and those whistles getting even closer.

"I'm not leaving him," Billy said.

Steve sighed. "Billy, there ain't no other way."

"He's—he's my friend. And I'm not leaving him behind. Not like Aoife. Not like Kayleigh. Not like Grandma..."

Steve looked down at him. He opened his mouth like he was going to say something reassuring. Something sympathetic.

And then he shook his head, and he sighed.

"I am sorry what you've been through, kid. And I'm sorry for what I'm gonna do next. But when you're alive in years to come... you'll thank me for it."

Billy frowned. "What—"

Before he knew it, Steve had hold of him.

Tight hold of him.

"Leave me!" Billy shouted, trying to kick and punch and scratch his way free of Steve's grip. "Let me go!"

"I'm sorry," Steve said as he dragged him up that ladder. Up towards the light. "I'm really sorry."

And Billy kept on trying to kick free. Kept on trying to shake free. Kept on trying to fight free. "Let me go!"

He kicked, and he punched, and he scratched, and he spat.

But in the end, it was no use.

Steve dragged him further and further up that ladder, out of the darkness, towards the light.

Down below, in that dark abyss, Rex stared up at him with those patient, wondering eyes.

That dangling tongue.

That wagging tail.

And it was only when Billy lost sight of him that he heard him begin to bark.

Just three barks.

A yelp.

A splash.

And then, silence.

CHAPTER TWENTY-SEVEN

Billy didn't say another word to Steve for the rest of the day.

It was late, and it was cold. They were in an old industrial unit. A warehouse of some kind. Looked like it'd been a delivery place once upon a time. Loads of big red postal vans were parked up inside. Some of the back doors had been broken into, parcels and letters tossed all over the place. Probably people searching for food deliveries inside those parcels. A reminder of the panic of the first days of darkness.

It was quiet in here. Billy had experienced silence a bunch of times since the blackout.

But right now, it felt even worse than ever.

Because of the absence of Rex's panting.

He felt his stomach turn when he thought of Rex.

Sitting there at the foot of the ladder.

Staring up at Steve and Billy as they disappeared towards the ground.

His three barks, and then the yelp.

And then the splash.

And then... nothing.

He shuddered when he thought about it. Shuddered when he thought about the smell of the sewers. Shuddered when he caught a whiff of it again, clinging to his skin. He tasted burning acid in his mouth. Wanted to throw up everywhere.

But he couldn't do anything but sit here, shivering in the darkness, convinced he should be resting or sleeping, unable to get any of it out of his head.

Kayleigh.

Rex.

Steve.

Mum...

None of it made sense.

None of it added up.

But it was all spiralling around his head.

It was all spiralling around his head, and it was all threatening to burst out, and he needed to take a deep breath, and he needed to get away and—

"Hey."

When Billy heard Steve's voice, it calmed him, just for a moment. It reminded him he wasn't alone.

And then when the implications started to sink in again—that this man had an affair with his mum, that this man was his actual dad—his panic picked up.

He turned away from Steve. Tried to zone out. Tried to go to that same place he went to when he was back with Ramiro.

The place where nothing mattered.

The place where he didn't care about anything.

The place where he felt dead...

But he couldn't. And that was his problem. He was *feeling* too much.

He tried to breathe, but he'd forgotten how to.

He crouched there on his knees, panting, heart racing, sweat drenching his body, and he gasped and gasped at the air.

"Hey," Steve said. Patting his back. "Listen to me. In through the nose. Slowly. Real slowly. Then hold it there. Hold it... hold it... and let go. Slowly. Slower than that. Okay. Now again. In through the nose..."

Billy breathed along. He was shaking. And he was terrified.

But he was still breathing. He hadn't forgotten how to.

He was okay after all.

"In... hold it... out. That's it. In... hold it... out."

He kept on going with this rhythm. And as much as he didn't know how he felt about Steve, as much as he was very, very confused about everything... he was beginning to feel a little better. A little calmer. A little more at ease.

Steve smiled when he looked up at him. "Good. That's better. You don't look like yer gonna drop dead on me any time soon n—"

Billy lunged at him. Punched him right across the face. Hard.

"Hey!" Steve said, touching his face. "What the hell was that for?"

"I've just lost my dog. I've just lost my friend. I've just found out my mum's dead and that you're... that you're my dad. And you're here acting like everything's normal. You're here making jokes. And—and it's not fair. It's just not fair."

Steve sighed. His mouth was actually bleeding a little. "You coulda just said that instead of punchin' me. I kinda saved your life back there."

Billy looked up at this man he barely even knew, and he shook his head. "If you're my... if you're my dad, then where were you? Where were you all my life?"

Steve tutted. Rolled his eyes. "Is this really the time for all this? Whistlers are out in full force out there, and you're choosing now to start solving all your family crap?"

"You said you were my dad. You said... you said my dad knew. That he knew I wasn't his boy. But if you knew... why didn't you do something? Why didn't you try to... Why did you just live down the road like everything was normal?"

Steve didn't answer right away. He just looked off into the darkness of this large, abandoned warehouse, and he sighed. "I thought about that a lot. A hell of a lot, I'll have you know. Keeps me awake at night. But in the end... I guess I just figured your ol' pa was probably better suited to raising a kid than I was. I didn't like the guy. Oliver was a right ol' prick to me, to your mother, and to you, too. But... but what you had there was a family unit. And I guess I worried."

"Worried?"

"What he might do if I tried to upset that family unit. To your mum. To... to you."

Billy looked into this man's eyes, and he saw it. He saw a flicker of himself, just for a second. An older version of himself, behind that beard, above those dark circles.

"This isn't... ideal," Steve said. "Nobody ever gets a manual on how to deal with these kinds of situations, right? But... but for what it's worth, I'm glad I found ya. I'm... I'm glad you came back home."

Billy looked away. His eyes were welling up.

"I'll never be your dad. I know that. Doesn't matter if I'm blood or not. I know family don't always work as neatly as that. But I... I do care, Billy. And I am sorry about what happened to your dog. And to your friend. But these people... these Whistlers... as much as you wanna get to them for it, you won't. Trust me. I've tried. I've tried, and it doesn't work that way."

"Tried by hiding underground in a sewer? Like a coward?"

Steve shrugged. "It is what it is. That's the shitty hand life dealt me. That's where I'm gonna go back when all this blows over. Or I'll find somewhere similar. Someplace safe. I'll be on the run from those fuckers for a long time. Especially after helpin' you out. But... But hey. That's life, right?"

Billy didn't know what to say. There were so many questions on his mind. "I saw her."

"Who?"

"I saw Mum. And I saw... I saw Kayleigh, too. I'm sure of it."

Steve looked away. A little shifty glance back at Billy, then away again.

"What do you know about that?"

"I don't know nothin' about that."

"You do. You're hiding something from me."

"I'm not hiding—"

"What do you know about—"

"I don't know a thing!" Steve shouted. "Okay? I don't know—I don't know a thing." His voice was shaky. His eyes were wide. He looked and sounded on the verge of tears. "But—but you need to stop pokin' your nose in things like that. They're gone, kid. I'm sorry. But they're gone. And the more you keep digging... the more you're gonna hurt yourself."

He stood up. Walked away from Billy, down those concrete steps, towards the vans.

"And you're just going to live this life?" Billy shouted.

Steve stopped. "Go to sleep."

Billy stood up. "You're just going to let them hunt you? Let them chase you? Let them punish you even though you haven't done a thing wrong?"

"I'm no saint."

"They can't get away with this. They can't keep hunting people. Keep killing people. And for what? All for what?"

Steve didn't answer. He just walked away.

Which made Billy even more suspicious.

"Do you ever tell the truth about anything?" Billy asked.

Steve stopped and turned around. And this time, he looked at Billy with a different look in his eyes.

With anger in his eyes.

"Don't go poking around where you're not welcome, son. It'll only get you hurt."

He looked at Billy a little longer than Billy was comfortable.

Then he turned around, and he walked down those steps.

"Get some sleep. You're gonna need it. And you'll feel better after it. I promise."

Billy watched him walk off towards those vans.

And then he saw him stop again. "And, um... it's good to see you. Really. I'm just sorry it ain't in better circumstances."

He glanced back at Billy.

Billy felt torn.

He felt conflicted.

But he took a deep breath, and he nodded.

"It's good to see you too."

Steve's eyes lit up.

Just for a second, a warm smile flickered across his face.

And then he walked off towards those vans again.

Billy felt bad.

He felt sorry for Steve.

Because he seemed a good man. He really did.

But one thing was for sure.

He wasn't staying here tonight.

He couldn't stay here tonight.

Because Steve was lying to him.

To protect him? Maybe. But lying all the same.

He looked out of the large window by his side.

Out over the industrial estate.

He was going to find Shelia.

He was going to find out what really happened to Kayleigh.

What happened to his mum.

And he was going to kill those responsible.

Once and for all.

CHAPTER TWENTY-EIGHT

Steve opened his eyes, and he knew something was wrong right away.

It was morning. Sunlight shone in through the large bay windows, many of them smashed. Dust particles bobbed around in the air. Up above, on the roof, pigeons flapped around, fluttering their wings. Rats of the sky, his dad used to always call them. But then he used to call squirrels the rats of the garden, too. Didn't really make much sense, seeing as Steve was pretty damned sure you got rats in gardens as well as squirrels. But hell. Maybe his old dad just had a thing with rats.

It looked sunny out. Bright. And that alone should've made him positive. Hopeful. Optimistic. Especially since his most recent discovery. Billy. His biological son...

He still couldn't believe he'd found him. That he'd been reunited... or rather, just *united* with him, after all these years. He'd never had a relationship with him. Never allowed himself to. Always afraid of getting too close to him because of Oliver, Kyla's husband. The man Billy called Dad.

And you know what? That arrangement kind of suited Steve. Because he didn't want a son. He didn't want no kids. He didn't want that level of responsibility. That was something he'd been dead certain about his whole life.

He thought about his dad getting the belt out.

Thought about him whipping him, right across the arse.

He wondered if that had anything to do with it.

But then he pushed that thought to one side. What did it matter anyway?

Now, he had Billy in his company. Now, he had a responsibility to him. A sense of duty to him. Whether he liked it or not.

But right now, he had a bad feeling. A real bad feeling.

A quietness to this place.

An emptiness...

He looked around the old warehouse. Listened to the echoing calls of the pigeons. The air was dusty. He was thirsty, and he was hungry. A smell of shit in the air, which he realised was probably him. Damn. He should really get changed after what happened in the sewers yesterday.

But then, who the hell was he trying to impress?

He thought about the sewers. Thought about what happened there. He'd called that place home for... well. For a while. Or rather, it was his bunker. It was his hideout. The double-decker above ground was far nicer in terms of its surroundings.

But he had to be sure nobody was around when he was up there.

That nobody was looking for him.

He looked around this empty warehouse, and he knew something was missing. And he had a nasty feeling in his gut that he knew exactly what it was that was missing.

Or *who* it was that was missing.

Billy.

He walked up the steps. Slowly. Right to where he'd left Billy last night. Right to where he'd told him to sleep.

There was no sign of Billy.

He was gone.

Steve stood there and looked down at the patch of floor where he'd lay. He had no idea how long he'd been gone. He had no idea *where* he'd gone. He just knew that this was always a possibility. This was always something he should've entertained. Always something he should've been worried about.

"Where'd you go to?" Steve muttered. "Where the hell'd you go to, kiddo?"

He walked over to the window. Looked outside. Looked at the industrial units all around this area. He looked at the trees in the distance.

And then he looked over in the direction of his old street.

He knew Billy didn't trust him. He knew he didn't believe him. Not completely.

But what was he supposed to tell Billy?

The truth?

The whole truth?

He'd already dropped enough of a bombshell on him. The kid needed to digest things before he told him anything else.

And yet...

Fuck. He wasn't giving up. That much was clear.

Steve stood at that window and looked outside. He felt sick. Didn't feel hungry anymore. His heart beat fast, so fast and strong that he could feel it, right the way through his body.

He stood there and stared outside, and he took a deep breath.

He didn't want to get drawn into a conflict.

He didn't want to end up fighting with an enemy he knew was way, way stronger than he could handle.

And he didn't want to have to look into the eyes of the people who did this.

The people who had taken Kyla from him.

He remembered how it ended, exactly how it ended... and he shivered.

He thought about what Billy said to him. How he'd seen his mum. And how he'd seen his friend, Kayleigh.

He hoped he wouldn't have to explain that to Billy.

And he hoped Billy wouldn't have to see it for himself.

He stood there. Swallowed a lump in his throat. Torn.

He'd been a loner. He'd been a loner for years now. So many years.

He'd always been a loner. And he'd preferred that life. A life of no responsibility.

He knew he could've been a better father.

He knew he could've been a better man.

He knew he could've stood up to Oliver and stopped him bullying Kyla, stopped him trying to turn his boy into something he'd never, ever turn him into, no matter how hard he tried.

His own biological flesh and blood.

He thought about Oliver, and his skin went cold.

He hoped Billy wouldn't find out about him.

Hoped he wouldn't discover the truth about him.

Poor kid could do without another bombshell to deal with.

He imagined what Kyla would say to him if she were still here. What she would want right now. More than anything.

And as scared as he felt, as weak as he felt... Steve knew he only had one choice.

He gathered his equipment.

He walked over towards the big metal doors of this industrial unit.

And he swallowed a lump in his throat again.

It was time to go after Billy.

It was time to help his son.

He owed him that much.

Billy stood over the manhole cover to the sewers and couldn't believe he was thinking of going down there again.

It was sunny, and it felt warm. There was a nice smell in the air. Like cut grass. Even though he knew nobody would be cutting any grass anywhere near here. Reminded him of Sunday mornings. Dad mowing the grass at Grandma's. Always smiled at Billy when he was doing it. Always seemed to be happy about it. He was always happiest at Grandma's. And he was always good to Billy there, too.

Probably because he knew how mean Grandma would be to him if he wasn't.

He thought about Grandma, and his stomach sank. Because if what Steve said was true... she *wasn't* his grandma. Not really. Who even was his real grandma? He didn't know. Didn't know a thing about Steve. Just that he was the man down the road.

The man down the road who'd had an affair with his mum.

The man down the road who was really his dad.

It was a lot to take in.

Billy was back at the manhole cover in the middle of the

street that Steve had dragged him out of. It was quiet. Nobody else around. No sounds other than a slight breeze. An old crisp packet scraping across the concrete. Abandoned cars. So many abandoned cars. Old plastic cups, which had once held beer. Cigarette butts everywhere. Looked like there might've been a party going on here, back when the lights went out.

It seemed weird. All these fossils of the old world still lying around, even though it was so many years ago now. And in a way, Billy felt like he wouldn't know what he'd do if the world went back to how it used to be. He felt like he wouldn't know how to behave or act.

Would anyone know how to behave anymore? How to act anymore?

He wasn't so sure.

He looked down at that manhole cover, and he thought about the last memory he had here.

Rex.

Rex's bark.

His yelp.

The splash, and then...

No.

He didn't want to think about what'd happened to Rex. He didn't want to think about him suffering or being hurt.

But he owed it to Rex to go down there.

To try and find him.

And after that?

He looked ahead. Looked down the street. Past the decaying, crumbling buildings. Off into the distance, into the empty haze.

He was going to find Sheila.

He was going to find her people.

And he was going to make them pay for the things they'd done.

He thought about Steve, and he felt bad for walking away from him. Abandoning him.

But then… Billy couldn't just give up like Steve had.

He couldn't just accept the people who had killed Mum were still out there. Going about their lives like normal. With no consequences.

And that Kayleigh was walking around with them…

He didn't get it. He just didn't understand.

Their crimes going completely unpunished.

Billy couldn't allow that. He couldn't live with that. He couldn't accept that.

He was going to hunt them down for it, and he was going to make them pay for it.

Dearly.

But first… Rex.

He took a deep breath. Looked back down at the manhole cover. He wasn't sure he wanted to climb back down into those sewers. Wasn't sure he could think of anything worse, in all truth. He'd just about got the stench of piss and shit from his nostrils after his last visit down there. The thought of going back down into that dark abyss again was just torture.

But this wasn't about what he liked and didn't like.

This was about being strong.

He went to lift that manhole cover when he heard something that froze him solid.

Behind him, he heard movement.

He heard footsteps.

And then he heard something that made all the hairs on his arms stand on end.

Growling.

CHAPTER THIRTY

Billy heard the movement and the growling right behind him, and he couldn't get one thought out of his mind.

Tiger.

It wouldn't be the first fucking time he'd come across a tiger in the wild. He remembered that day a month ago, that awful day when Aoife died.

And it didn't feel real when that happened. It felt like he was in a dream. Or a nightmare. But he knew there were zoo animals out there. And he knew there would be more of them, too.

He stood there, frozen, heart racing, and he had to prepare himself for whatever he was about to face right now.

The sun beamed down brightly from above. His skin felt hot, clammy. He saw the manhole cover Steve had dragged him up from last night as they ran away from Sheila and her people. The manhole cover he wanted to search beneath. Because it was the last place he'd seen Rex. The last place he'd heard him.

And as he stood there, frozen, he thought about lurching forward. About lifting that cover.

Because it might be the only way to escape whatever was behind him.

Whatever was coming for him.

He stood there, totally still, and he heard that noise again.

That growl. Right behind him.

So close.

It didn't sound like a tiger. Didn't sound as loud as a tiger. Maybe something smaller. Maybe a wolf.

Or...

He stood there totally rooted to the spot. Shaking. He could smell something that smelled like wee, and he wondered if it was him, unable to keep it in, unable to stop himself. He tasted sick in his dry mouth. He couldn't just stand here. He had to turn around. He had to look. He had to see.

He closed his eyes, took a deep breath, and prepared himself to face whatever fate awaited him.

And then he turned around.

He didn't see it at first. Just the pavement. Just the buildings all boarded up, the wood over the windows torn away and rotting, now.

He wondered if the tiger had torn at the wood.

Or something worse than the tiger.

The monster.

The monster, finally catching up with him, once and for all...

He stood there, shaking. Swallowing a big lump in his throat.

The growling had stopped.

And he couldn't see what its source was.

He couldn't see where it came from.

A thought came to mind.

A momentary thought flashing up in his head.

Run.

Run while you can.

He held his breath and clenched his fists.

No growling.

Still no growling.

And then when he finally found the courage to turn around...

he heard it.

A bark.

A deep, angry, aggressive bark.

A dog or a wolf.

He didn't even think anymore.

He just ran.

He ran down the street. Ran past the old cars. Ran over the smashed glass. He could hear footsteps chasing him, pelting after him, getting quicker and quicker, closing in...

He wanted to look back.

Wanted to see how far away it was.

But at the same time, he needed to keep looking ahead.

Keep his focus ahead.

He saw a big house ahead, with grey walls. There were big trees in the garden. Really long grass out front, too. And a few broken windows.

If he could get in there... maybe, he could hide.

Maybe he could lay low and hide and...

He heard barking.

Even closer now.

He looked around.

Turned around and looked, even though he knew he probably shouldn't.

Even though he knew it was dangerous.

He glanced around and saw movement behind him.

Movement getting closer.

A dark shadow of movement—

He felt something hit his right foot.

Felt his balance wavering.

And before he could do anything, before he could stop himself, he tripped up and slammed face first against the ground.

His hands grazed right against the concrete. They stung like mad. He tasted blood in his mouth from where he'd bitten his tongue. His head spun, and he felt sick.

But he didn't have any time to think.

Because those footsteps.

And that barking...

He wanted to give up.

He wanted to curl up into a ball and cry...

No.

You're stronger than that, Billy.

You've always been stronger than that.

He gritted his teeth, and he turned around, knife in hand.

He was going to stand up to whatever was chasing him.

He was going to fight it if he had to.

He was going to...

He froze.

He saw the beast standing over him.

Growling.

Drooling.

Its fur looked matted. It looked damp, and it smelled like a sewer. There was a bit of a patch on its back where its fur looked like it'd been hacked at and a nasty bloody wound.

It wasn't a beast.

It wasn't an *it*.

"Rex," Billy said.

And right then, Billy didn't care that Rex had literally been in a sewer. He didn't care about any of that.

All he cared about was the fact that Rex was here.

He was alive.

"Come here, Rex."

Rex collided with him. A little nervous. A little hesitant, more so than usual.

But it was him.

It was him, and he was here, and he was cuddling him.

And he didn't care about his smell.

He didn't care about how much he was hurting himself.

He didn't care about anything.

Just that he was here.

He held him tight. Pulled back. Saw that nasty wound on his back. And he felt bad for him. So sorry for him.

"I'm sorry, lad. I'm—I'm sorry for leaving you down there."

Rex just let out a little grunt. A little contented grunt.

"I won't leave you again. And—and I won't give up on you or anyone again. Anyone. Ever."

Rex grunted again, almost in acknowledgement.

He held his breath, and he thought about Steve. He thought about what he'd said about Mum. And then about Kayleigh too, and how he swore he'd seen her down in the sewers.

He thought about Sheila. And what she'd done.

He thought about all these things. And as much as he wanted to disappear, as much as he wanted to walk away with Steve... at the same time, he didn't.

Because he wanted to stand up to Sheila.

He wanted to fight her.

He wanted to stop this madness.

And there was something else, too.

Mum.

Mum and Kayleigh.

Steve wasn't being completely straight with him about them.

He didn't know what, and he didn't know why... but something just wasn't right.

He stood up. Rex by his side. He tensed his bleeding, shaking fists. And he looked down the car-filled road and off into the horizon.

"Come on, Rex," he said. "It's time to go back home again."

It was time to finish this.

He took a deep breath.

Thought of Steve.

Felt bad, just for a second.

And then, with Rex by his side, Billy walked.

CHAPTER THIRTY-ONE

Sheila stood in the old, derelict house and watched Billy through the window.

It was a nice day. A real pretty day, in all truth. The morning breeze was warm against her skin. It reminded her why spring was her favourite season. Always had been. Sure, summer was nice. But seeing life return was a big reason why spring appealed to her so much.

It was the season Lucia spoke of, too.

The season Lucia always prophesied about.

The season Lucia claimed all the best things would happen.

That all the greatest luck would arrive.

And looking out this window at Billy, now?

She started to believe Lucia was right all along.

The street outside was quiet otherwise. The usual sights. The smashed windows, some of them boarded up. The graffiti on the roof of the house opposite: HELP.

Smeared in something red. Blood? Quite possibly.

And the thing that always got to Sheila, more than anything? How desensitised you could become to it all. How ordinary the silence felt now. She'd never forget what that first lockdown felt like during the COVID days—the days that seemed so long ago.

She'd never forget walking off into the countryside, over to the motorway bridge near where she lived and standing on it. Looking down at that empty motorway. The occasional car flying past. But not many. So, so few.

And as much as it was a time of horror... there was something *nice* about it.

Something relaxed about it.

It was like Earth had restored itself to the way it should be. A chance for a great reset, one so desperately needed, in the wake of climate change, natural disaster, ecological collapse, and all those things.

But then, of course, things had gone back to normal. The status quo *had* returned, as much as people claimed it wouldn't.

People went back to the office.

People started hanging out in their droves again.

People forget that connection with nature. They forgot who their master really was, even though they'd been faced with it in the least subtle way.

And it infuriated Sheila.

She didn't want to think about her life before.

She didn't want to get trapped in that ruminative hellscape.

Because life was better now.

She was stronger now.

She had Lucia beside her, at last.

She thought about how she'd formed her community. How they'd found each other in the early days and how things were quite normal.

And then how things got more... interesting as time went by.

More prophetic.

How everything they did was in the service of a higher power. Of Lucia.

And how it excused some of their worst behaviours.

How it gave them the justification they needed for doing some horrible, horrible things.

But there was still a piece of the puzzle missing.

A final piece.

Billy.

And now he was right here, and a whole new era was about to begin.

She looked out that broken window at Billy and the dog, and she smiled. She knew he'd come back here. Didn't matter what the tramp told him or where he took him. She could see that strength in his eyes. That lust for vengeance in his eyes.

She knew he was a kid who wouldn't give up.

And the cruel irony of it all?

He thought that made him *strong* somehow.

When, in fact, it made him weak.

It was going to prove his greatest weakness.

She heard footsteps. Looked around this dark, dusty bedroom. Over the old bed, covered in mould and pigeon shit. It was so grim in here. Shit all over the carpet, which looked like it was cream once upon a time. Little beetles creeping around underneath the bed. In the corner of the room, a dead rat, lying on its back, little paws poking up into the air. It had a chunk of its fur ripped away, its bright red innards on show, spilling out like wriggly worms.

It reeked. Reeked in here.

But Sheila was used to that now.

She was used to all of it.

She looked to the back of the room, and she saw Calvin standing there holding something important in hand.

Something she was going to find very, very useful.

He looked at her with those big, cold eyes. He didn't say a word to her. He didn't have to.

She walked over to him. Walked past more of her people,

sitting against the walls of this place. All so silent. All so composed. All so compliant.

And she took the item from Calvin's hands.

Smiled at him.

Nodded.

And then she walked over to the window.

She looked back out. Out of the cool darkness of this room and into the warm light.

Looked at Billy.

Looked at the dog.

It would be time for him to discover the truth soon.

The whole truth.

The truth of Lucia.

The truth of why she was pursuing him so dearly.

The truth behind *everything*.

She held her breath and looked out that window, right at them.

And then she lifted the item to her face and stretched it around her skin like a mask.

Like a comfy pair of slippers.

She tightened the strings around the back of her head. Looked out through the eyeholes.

And she smiled.

She knew what she had to do.

She knew exactly what she had to do.

CHAPTER THIRTY-TWO

Billy stood in the middle of his old street and couldn't shake the feeling he was being watched.

It had to be late morning now. It was warm. Really warm. Felt like a summer's day, only not such a nice one. Too stuffy. Too humid. He always used to want to wear his shorts for school when it was like this. But Dad told him his shorts looked stupid. Told him they made him look like a "puff."

So he just went along with what his dad said. Even though he didn't see what was wrong with "puffs" as Dad called them, or why their preferences made them any stronger or weaker.

He went along with what he suggested, with his trousers on, stuck to his legs, drenched in sweat. Something the other kids teased him about.

It was a choice between being teased by the other kids for not wearing shorts or being teased by Dad for wearing shorts.

Anything that kept Dad off his case was always better.

He stood on his road and looked down at the terraced houses. The row he used to live at. He saw Steve's house, a few doors down from his. He wondered how many times he'd walked past that house with no idea about the truth of the man in there... or rather, the truth *he* told him, anyway.

He shivered at the thought. He didn't want to think about that.

The main thing was... right now, he was here.

He was here, and he had questions.

He looked over at that big semi-detached house on the side of the road opposite his, and his stomach turned.

That was the last place he'd seen Kayleigh, before... well, before *whatever* happened to her. He didn't know what'd happened to her. Assumed she'd been killed at first. But now, he wasn't sure.

He'd seen her. He didn't care what Steve said. He'd seen her face in those sewers. Just like he'd seen Mum's face in his garden.

Steve was hiding something from him. He didn't know what. And he didn't know why.

But he was here for answers.

The street was quiet. No movement at all. Which made it creepier. On a normal summer or spring day—a sunny day like this —kids would be biking up and down the street all the time. Laughing amongst themselves. Joking together. The smell of barbecues in the air. The sound of the ice cream van approaching...

But now, it was silent. It was dead.

It was weird being back here. Because it didn't feel like home anymore. Not without all the other things that used to come with home, the things that made it home.

If he hadn't seen Mum in the back yard, he would've concluded that it was a waste of time coming back here. Because he hadn't found anything he wanted to find at all.

And worse than that. He'd lost Kayleigh here.

And he'd found out the horrible truth about his mum and Steve.

A truth he was still battling to wrap his head around.

He stood in the middle of the street, Rex wagging his tail by his side, and he took a deep breath. At least Rex was here with him. He was so grateful for that. Still didn't think it was real. Thought he was dreaming.

He smiled at Rex. "Better go take a look, hadn't we?"

And then they walked down the street. His footsteps and Rex's panting were the only sounds. That and the crows. Always crows, sitting there on the roofs of the houses.

Staring down at him.

Watching him.

Cawing so loud.

Like they were the guards of this place.

Like they were the eyes of the monster, watching his every step.

He walked over towards his old house. He'd been back there once already. Had a proper look around it. What was he expecting to find there?

But still. He had to go in there. He'd seen Mum. There had to be a trace of her in there or around there. He had to look harder.

He stopped when he reached Steve's house.

He stood there. Looked at the door. The brown wood chipped away. The gnomes in the yard all cracked and broken. He looked at the windows, all steamed up and dusty, impossible to see inside.

What if there was something in there?

What if there was some kind of truth in there that he just hadn't seen yet?

He looked towards that dark, dingy window, and he started to walk towards it, when he heard movement behind him.

He turned around. Lifted his knife.

There was no movement in the street.

Those stationary cars.

Those empty windows.

And those crows, staring down at him.

Watching.

"You see anything, Rex?" he asked.

But of course, Rex didn't respond. He was a dog. What was Billy expecting?

He stared across the sun-drenched street. Made sure he didn't see any movement. Went to turn back to Steve's house again.

And just as he went to turn, he saw it.

Movement.

Someone running into that house.

The tall, grey-bricked house.

The one where Kayleigh had fired bullets from the windows.

The last place he'd seen her.

His stomach tensed. He'd been trying to avoid that place.

But seeing this figure.

Seeing her run towards that house.

And there was something that made him even more alarmed.

Kayleigh.

It was her.

He recognised her blonde hair.

He recognised her face.

There was something... different about her. Just like there was something different about her when he'd seen her in the sewers. He wasn't sure. Maybe he was just remembering her wrong.

But there was absolutely no doubt about it in Billy's mind.

This was Kayleigh.

He walked across the quiet, empty street. Crows still staring down, still cawing away. Watching. Like they were waiting for him to make his discovery, too.

He looked to his left. To his right. The wind was picking up.

He swore he heard whispers in that breeze.

Swore he heard whistling in the emptiness.

He turned ahead and saw it again.

There was someone in the window of that house, right upstairs.

Staring out at him one second.

Then disappearing the next.

"Kayleigh," he said.

He walked slowly across the street. Held that knife so tightly he felt it might break in his hand.

What was she doing?

Why was she running away from him?

Why was she hiding?

He reached the opposite side of the street.

Stood there.

Stood and stared at the door to that house.

It was open now.

It was ajar.

Someone was here.

He looked at the darkness beyond the door. At the dust and the debris on the floor. And he knew there was no backing out now.

He knew he had to go in there.

He knew he had to investigate it in there.

He knew he had to see what was in there for himself.

He took a deep breath.

Swallowed a lump in his throat.

You can do this, Billy.

You owe it to her to do this.

He walked up to the door when he heard something.

Something that sent a shiver up his spine.

A whistle.

Someone whistling over to his left.

He looked around. The hairs on the back of his neck standing right on end.

The Whistlers.

Was it them?

Or was it just the wind?

In the distance, he didn't see a thing.

He just saw the same stationary cars.

The same houses.

The same lack of movement, and the same silence.

He turned back around to the front door.

Lifted his knife, just in case.

"Now or never," he said.

And then he pushed the door open.

The door creaked as he moved it. There was something behind it, blocking him from opening it fully.

He looked inside. Held on to his knife.

He had to be ready for someone to jump out.

He had to be ready for anything.

He looked inside. There were loads of debris around the floor. Photographs that had once been on the walls were smashed on the wooden flooring. A dark wooden cabinet lay flat on its front. A vase smashed in front of him.

He walked in slowly. His footsteps echoing. Every sound was louder in here. His breathing. Rex's panting.

And hopefully... whoever was in here.

But he couldn't hear them anymore.

They were silent.

He looked around this downstairs area. Looked at the dust floating in the air. He looked at the photos on the wall. Mrs Richards, who used to live here. Happy photos with her boys. Nowhere near capturing the painful upbringing she had raising them.

He looked at her smile, and he hoped wherever she was, she was happy now.

Away from the neighbours who hated her.

He wanted to look more around this house when he heard the movement upstairs.

He looked at the stairs. Looked at the dirty footprints on the cream carpet, the one Mrs Richards loved so much. He pictured how annoyed she would be at those prints. How angry they would make her.

Wherever she was... he hoped she wouldn't come back here to see them.

He started climbing then. Climbing the stairs. Climbing them towards those noises.

That shuffling.

Someone moving around.

Someone—

Outside, another whistle.

He spun around.

Looked over at the front door.

Did he just see someone?

Someone racing in front of the door?

Rex whined. Wagged his little doggy tail. But even he looked a bit nervous.

"It's okay," Billy said. "We're... we're almost there."

He looked up the stairs.

Up towards the landing area.

The stairs that the two brothers, Brendan and Dave, used to play on all those years ago.

The one Brendan pushed Dave down once. Smiled when he did it.

And Dave didn't see that it was wrong. He just laughed along, too.

If he was laughing... was it so bad, really?

He reached the top of the stairs when he froze.

The door.

The door to the bedroom.

The one Kayleigh was in.

The one she'd fired those bullets from.

It was moving.

Closing.

Like someone had just been in there and pushed it shut behind them.

He swallowed a lump in his throat again.

Took a deep breath.

He didn't know what he would come across.

He didn't know what he would face.

But he had to be ready.

He walked to the door with that knife in his hand.

Heart racing.

Chest tight.

What are you doing here, Billy?

What the hell are you doing here?

And then he took another deep breath and pushed that door open.

He looked inside.

Saw the foot of a bed.

Saw more dust everywhere.

And dirty footprints on that cream carpet...

Wait. No. Not dirt.

Blood.

Bloody footprints.

He wasn't sure how long he stood at the entrance to that door. Just standing there. Knife gripped tight in his shaking hand.

But he knew he couldn't hide from the truth much longer.

He closed his eyes.

He took another deep breath.

And then he stepped into that room.

The first thing he noticed was the bed.

Or rather, what was on the bed.

When he saw what was on the bed, he stopped.

He stood still.

Completely still.

Stared over at it.

Speechless.

Voiceless.

Unable to comprehend what he was looking at.

Unable to think.

Billy didn't regret coming back here.

Not until that moment.

But right now, looking at what he was seeing...

He felt afraid.

Very afraid.

CHAPTER THIRTY-THREE

Billy stared ahead at the bed in front of him and tried to understand what he was looking at.

It was warm in this room. So warm. His cheeks felt hot, even though the room was in the shade.

The room was dark. The curtains were only partly open. But enough light crept in for him to see what was on the bed.

For him to take it in.

To wrap his head around it.

To understand.

He looked at the bed and clenched his fists together. He started shaking. His heart started racing, faster and faster and faster.

Because of what he was looking at.

It made him understand.

Made him see that what he'd feared all along was true.

A woman was sitting on the bed. She had her hands on her legs. She was still. Totally still.

Billy could tell from her body and what she was wearing that it was Kayleigh.

And it was a good job he could tell it was Kayleigh from her body and her clothes.

Because he definitely couldn't tell from her face.

She didn't have a face.

Not anymore.

There was a bloody, red blot where her face once was. Right down to the neck. Blood had splattered all over her white shirt and the wall behind her.

And he could see her skull.

He could see her facial muscles.

He could see those eyes staring out of those sockets, so wide.

A wide mouth.

Like it was screaming.

And a bald head, but for a few bleached blonde strands.

He tasted vomit. Went to hurl up as Rex stood beside him. Swallowed it back down. He walked towards her. Then he stepped back. Not understanding. Not realising how this could be possible.

Flies.

Flies buzzing around her.

The smell of fresh meat like a butcher's market.

Those wide blue eyes glaring back at him in horror.

That...

He heard it, then.

A creak.

A creaking of a floorboard right beside him.

And as he stood there, shaking, he had a sudden, horrifying realisation.

There was someone in here with him.

He heard the floorboards creaking. And he could hear breathing, too. Breathing, right behind him.

Rex by his side.

Growling.

He didn't want to turn around. He didn't want to look. He didn't want to see.

Because as much as he didn't want to accept it, as much as he didn't want to see it for himself... he had a bad feeling about what he was going to see.

He had a bad feeling because deep down, he knew what he was going to see.

But he was going to have to look anyway.

He was going to have to force himself to look.

Whether he liked it or not.

He heard Rex's growling.

He heard that heavy breathing.

Look, Billy.

You've seen the worst things in the world already.

One of them is right in front of you, lying on that bed.

Just look...

He closed his eyes.

Took a deep breath.

And he turned around.

When he looked around, he saw someone standing there.

It was a man.

Well. They had the body of a man. The thick legs. The muscular, tattooed arms.

Only...

There was something about this man that was different.

And that was his face.

It was then that Billy tasted vomit in his mouth even more.

That he wanted to throw up everywhere.

Because he saw exactly whose face it was.

It was Kayleigh's' face.

Her face had been torn away like a mask from her skull.

And now it had been tied around this man's head.

As had her blonde hair.

Blonde hair splattered with bright red blood.

The man stood there and stared at Billy.

And Billy stared back at him.

And suddenly, it caught up with him.

Suddenly it all made sense.

Why he'd seen Kayleigh in the sewers, only with something *off* about her.

Why Steve had been so reluctant to tell him the truth.

And Mum...

No.

No, they can't have done this to Mum.

Mum can't have met the same fate.

He stood there, and he just knew he had to get away.

He knew he had to run.

Or fight.

He saw the man standing there. Breathing heavily. And outside, he heard whistling.

Whistling, getting closer.

Whistling in the street.

These people were here.

This was a trap, and they were here.

He looked at the door beside the man.

Then back at the man.

Then he tightened his grip around the knife again.

He held the man's gaze. Staring through the sockets where Kayleigh's eyes once were. Speechless.

And then he went to lift his knife—

Before he could do anything about it, the man grabbed his arm.

He yanked it back.

Then he pushed Billy down onto the bed.

Right between Kayleigh's cold, dead legs.

He stared down at Billy.

Stood right over him as Rex barked like mad at him,

As those whistles got closer.

And then his smile widened.

Or rather, Kayleigh's smile widened.

He went to lift his hands, and as much as Billy wanted to be strong, as much as he wanted to stand up, as much as he wanted to fight, there was only one thing he could do.

Close his eyes and pray he disappeared, as the whistles got louder and louder and...

CHAPTER THIRTY-FOUR

Billy did the only thing he could do as he lay down on that bed, a man with Kayleigh's face standing over him.

He squeezed his eyes shut, and he prayed.

He stared into the blinding darkness. Time stood completely still. He could hear Rex barking away by the side of the bed, feel the weight of the bed shifting as that man got closer and closer to him.

And he could smell it.

He could smell that rotting, sour stench right behind him.

The stench of Kayleigh's body.

Her cold legs like a mannequin dummy either side of him.

Totally still.

He lay there, and he didn't want to open his eyes. He was too afraid to open his eyes. Too afraid to look up at the person standing over him.

But then he remembered something else.

He remembered that strength inside him.

He remembered how angry he was at these people for what they'd done to him.

For what they'd taken away from him.

And he remembered the promise he'd made to Rex.

To be there for him.

To fight for him.

He swallowed a lump in his throat—swallowed down the fear —and he opened his eyes.

He saw the man standing over him, in all his horrifying glory, once again.

He saw his bright blue eyes piercing through those sockets.

He saw the pale skin of Kayleigh's face, stretched across that man's head, which looked too big to take it.

He saw the dead expression on her cracked lips.

And he felt a total, unshakable sense of fear.

But he took a breath.

He took a breath, and he dragged himself up.

He went to swing that knife at the man when he realised something.

Blood.

Blood drooling from Kayleigh's lips.

No.

Not from Kayleigh's lips.

From the *man's* lips.

It dribbled out over Kayleigh's chin. Right down her face. And then he started coughing. He started gargling. Shaking. Contorting.

And all this time, Billy could hear those whistles.

He could hear the whistles outside getting closer and closer, and...

The man clutched his neck. And then he grabbed the skin at his chin. Kayleigh's skin.

He peeled it away from his face like it was some sort of rubber mask, and Billy saw more blood come pooling out from his throat.

He noticed something else, too, as he lay there between

Kayleigh's limp legs and stared up at that man as he struggled and gargled for breath.

Rex.

Rex wasn't barking anymore.

He was panting.

Like he did when he was relaxed.

And then, out of nowhere, the man's eyes rolled back into his skull, and he fell forward.

Almost fell onto Billy, who had to scramble out of the way to stop him landing on him.

Blood pooled out over the dusty sheets. Dark red blood mixing with Kayleigh's blood, which already covered it.

And then Billy saw him.

The man standing over the one wearing Kayleigh's face.

The man standing there, knife in his hand, and staring right at Billy.

"You were stupid for comin' back here, kiddo," Steve said. "Real, real stupid."

Billy was surprised to see Steve. Surprised he'd followed him. But then, he had a sense that he was being watched for quite a while now.

And now they were here, he felt relieved. On the one hand, relieved because he'd bailed him out.

On the other... a little aggrieved that he hadn't been able to prove himself.

To prove his own strength.

To himself.

But then he heard those whistles. Heard them getting closer. Heard them right outside the house.

"We've gotta move," Steve said, grabbing Billy's arm, dragging him to his feet. "Those nutters are crawling around this place."

And Billy had questions. He had questions about Kayleigh. About what they'd done to her.

And he had questions about Mum. Whether she'd faced the same fate.

Seeing her in the garden and something being... *off* about her.

Just like something seemed off about the Kayleigh he'd seen in the sewers.

Goosepimples spread across his skin.

He had so, so many questions.

But as he looked back at Kayleigh's limp body lying there on the bed, her face torn from her flesh... and then at the man lying before her. Bleeding out everywhere. The smell of rusty metal strong in the air... as he looked back at this horror scene, he just wanted to get away from here.

Questions could wait.

It was time to go.

"Now!" Steve said.

They ran. Ran out onto the landing area. Ran towards those creaky, dusty stairs. Back towards the front door. The sooner they got out of this place, the better. The sooner they got out of this place...

Billy stopped.

There were people at the door.

People coming through the door.

"Back up the stairs," Steve said, dragging him backwards.

He ran. He had no choice. He didn't want to stay up here, but what other choice did he have?

"What now?" Billy asked.

"We're—we're gonna have to go out one of the windows. Bathroom, maybe."

Billy felt his stomach sink as those whistles and those footsteps raced after them. "Why's it always the bloody bathroom window?"

"What?"

He shook his head. "Nothing."

He ran through the bathroom door. Went to close it, shut.

He saw two of them at the top of the stairs.

Two of them wearing faces he didn't recognise.

Long, greasy hair dangling down from their heads.

Whistling in this haunting, high-pitched way that sent shivers creeping up his skin.

"Billy!"

Billy knew he had no more time to wait.

He slammed the door shut.

And then he ran over to the other side of the bathroom.

Much to his relief, Steve was already at the window.

And there was something there that made him even happier.

Even more grateful.

Made him realise he was even more fortunate than usual.

"Scaffolding," Billy said.

"Down here. We've got to go, Billy. We've got a chance to get out of here, and we've got to take it. Now."

He went to run when he heard the door bang open behind him.

And he knew he had no choice then.

He ran across the bathroom. Past the free-standing bath, filled with dirt and grime. Past the shower, covered in thick green mould. He ran as fast as he could away from those footsteps and away from those whistles, and then he jumped through the open window.

Jumped onto that scaffolding.

Steve beside him.

Rex beside him.

He turned around.

Turned around and went to slam the window shut to buy them a bit more time.

"No time, Billy," Steve said. "There's no…"

Billy didn't hear what else he said.

He looked through that window, and he saw her standing there.

She was right by the bathroom door.

Standing still. Totally still.

And when Billy looked at her, he didn't realise who she was. Not for a moment.

And then it clicked.

It all clicked in a horrifying flash.

It was Sheila.

The leader of these people.

She was standing there holding a knife.

Only there was something different about her.

Something that set Billy's hairs on end.

Something that made him want to disappear into a hole in the ground.

Sheila wasn't just Sheila.

Sheila was wearing someone's face.

Sheila was wearing the face of someone he recognised.

Someone he recognised very, very well.

Sheila was wearing Mum's face.

CHAPTER THIRTY-FIVE

Billy had seen some horrible things in his time.

He'd seen blood. He'd seen suffering. He'd seen death.

He'd seen and been through the absolute worst anyone could ever go through.

Pain.

Loss.

Torment.

But looking at his mum's face stretched across Sheila's like a rubber mask right now... he wasn't sure he'd ever seen anything that made him feel so much pain.

Clouds covered the burning sun. Little specks of cold rain fell from above. Billy stood on that scaffolding at the back of the house, right outside the bathroom window. He stared in through that window. Towards Sheila, who stood there.

Stood there, totally still.

Stood there, holding a knife.

Stood there, with Mum's face covering hers.

Smiling.

He could hear Rex growling somewhere. And he could hear

Steve shouting things at him, too. Urging him to hurry. Grabbing his wrist and trying to pull him down the scaffolding.

But Billy wasn't going anywhere.

How *could* he go anywhere?

He could only stand and stare at this woman as she stood there with his mum's face wrapped over hers and feel all kinds of emotions raging in his body.

Anger.

Pain.

Sadness.

Despair.

Hatred.

"Billy," Steve said. "I—I'm sorry. I—"

"You said she died in your arms," Billy said. He wasn't really thinking about what he was saying. Wasn't thinking about anything at all right now.

"I'm sorry, Billy. We—we can talk about it some other time. Just not right now. There—there won't be another time if you don't get a move on. You need to listen to me, Billy. Seriously. You need to hear me..."

But Billy didn't hear him.

He couldn't hear anything.

He couldn't see anything.

Nothing but Sheila.

Nothing but Mum's face.

Nothing but those whistles, getting louder and louder in his skull.

His anger, building and building and building...

"Your friend was lucky," Sheila said. "The one who we dealt with in this very building. She didn't exactly have... a nice exit. But we made it relatively pain-free. Relatively."

Billy's fists tightened.

His anger built up.

"Billy," Steve said. "Don't listen to them. Please."

"I mean, it could've been easier on her," Sheila said. "If you'd been stronger. If you hadn't run away from her like a scared little boy."

"I'm not a scared little boy," Billy spat.

"Really? You really think not? Look at you. Running away from us again. Even when I'm standing here and wearing poor Kyla's face…"

"Don't you say her name," Billy said, lunging forward.

"Billy," Steve said. "No. Don't—don't do it. She wants you to react. Understand? She wants you to react."

Sheila's smile widened some more. Billy swore he could hear the whistling getting louder. But he didn't know if it was outside, around the street, or in his head… all in his head…

Kill her.

Make her pay.

Show your strength.

"Speaking of your mother," Sheila said. Walking closer to that bathroom window. Slowly. "What I just said about your friend… I can't say the same for her."

Billy's gut turned.

He felt dizzy.

He felt sick.

"We kept her alive for a long time," Sheila said. "Or rather… Lucia did. Because she was special to Lucia. Extra, extra special."

Billy's head shook as his pulse raced through it.

As Sheila got closer.

"And whatever our traitor here told you… whatever he tells himself to make himself sleep easier at night… he'll never hide away from the fact he is a coward. And that you are a coward. Just like him."

Billy looked around at Steve then. He didn't understand any of it. Couldn't wrap his head around any of it.

But he needed answers.

He needed to understand.

He needed *something*.

"He was one of us," Sheila said. "And he walked away. All got too much for him, and he walked. Left your dear mother behind, though. Left her in her rightful place on the throne. All because he couldn't kneel to Lucia. All because he couldn't bring himself to give up his pride. He ran away. Like a weak, weak little man he is. And now look at you both. Bound in weakness together."

Billy looked at Steve. And he didn't even have to ask him whether this was true for him to know.

He saw the way Steve lowered his head.

Saw the tears in his bloodshot eyes.

"I didn't want to leave her," he said. "If—if I'd known what was gonna happen... I wouldn't have left her."

The shit about her dying in his arms.

All of it was a lie.

She'd died on her own.

Died in pain.

Because Steve was a coward.

And he was Billy's dad.

A coward's dad.

"She was alive a long time afterwards," Sheila said.

Billy spun around.

Stared into those eyes as she got closer.

As his mother's face got closer.

That little freckle under her right eye, right on her cheek.

"And you know what she kept saying, even after we'd peeled her skin from her face?"

"Stop," Billy said. Heart racing faster. Chest tighter. Body shaking. Knees weak.

Sheila took another step closer to Billy. So close to that bathroom window now.

"You know what she kept saying to us? What the last thing she said to us was?"

"Don't listen to her, Billy," Steve shouted. He sounded further away. So too did Rex, who was barking away. "Don't listen to her!"

Sheila was so close to Billy now.

Her face so close.

Mum's face so close.

She looked at Billy with those bright blue eyes and on that hard face, a smile.

"She kept on saying she wished someone would help her. She wished someone in her life was strong enough to help her. That they weren't weak. That they weren't weak like you."

He knew he should stand his ground.

Logically, he knew Steve was right.

He knew he shouldn't lunge at Sheila.

He knew she was trying to goad him.

But seeing her standing there, wearing Mum's face.

After everything she'd done.

After everything her people had done.

He just couldn't hold back anymore.

He threw himself back through the window.

"Billy, no!" Steve shouted.

And as he jumped through, he lifted his knife.

He pulled it back.

He went to swing it at Sheila, and he felt something from his right.

Something knock him to his back.

Something send him flying to the cold, tiled bathroom floor.

Another one of Sheila's people.

Hiding by the side of the window.

"Billy!" Steve shouted.

He heard Steve shouting. He heard the whistling getting louder.

He looked up, and he saw Sheila standing over him.

Smile on her face.

Knife in hand.

He tried to wriggle free as he felt those hands pinning him to the floor.

He tried to kick and punch and shake himself out of this bind.

He tried, and he tried, and in the end, he didn't stop trying.

Sheila crouched down.

Crouched right over him.

She pulled Mum's face back, just a little, so it wasn't covering her mouth. Not anymore.

And then she looked down at her with little specks of old, grey flesh covering her chin.

Smile on her face.

"Well done, Billy," she said. "You belong to Lucia now."

CHAPTER THIRTY-SIX

Billy sat in the darkness, and weirdly, he felt at home here.

He had no idea what time of day it was. He had no idea how long he'd been in here. He had no idea about anything at all. He didn't know what the weather was like outside. He didn't know whether he was in a building or a shed or if he was buried underground.

All he knew was that he was back where he belonged.

Right back where he belonged.

Back in captivity.

Back in the darkness.

Back without hope.

He looked around and saw nothing. Nothing at all. And it was always this way. Just perfect jet black. He didn't hear anything, either. The Whistlers had put earplugs into his ears. So he didn't even know if he was alone in here or with other people.

Every now and then, he swore he heard movement. Shuffling beside him. Then he realised it was probably just his heart. His pulse whooshing through his skull.

Whispers.

Whispers in his head, all the time.

They killed her.

They killed Kayleigh, and they killed your mum, and you did nothing to help.

Nobody did a thing to help.

She suffered.

She died alone.

She died in pain, and she died scared and—

No!

He clenched his eyes shut. He wanted to shout. Wanted to scream. But his mouth was gagged. They'd shoved a rag in his mouth so far that it kept touching the back of his sore, dry throat, making him heave every now and then, making his eyes constantly water. He worried about leaning back. Or even falling asleep. He worried that rag might slip into his throat, and he might choke.

And there was nothing he could do about it.

Nothing he could do about it because of his hands tied behind his back.

His ankles tied together.

Trapped.

Completely trapped.

He sat there in the darkness. His nose was blocked, and he could only just breathe through his nostrils. The room smelled of damp. But he was used to it by now.

Used to the smell of damp.

Used to the taste of blood.

Used to that freezing cold feeling, right through his shaking body.

And even though he was here—even though he was trapped here—mentally, he was somewhere else. He was somewhere else entirely.

He was back there on that scaffolding, staring in through that window.

Steve by his side.

He thought about Steve. The look of shame on his face when Sheila told Billy what really happened to Mum. He'd lied to Billy. Why? To protect him, probably.

But knowing the truth hadn't protected him.

Being hidden from the truth had made it even worse when he found out.

He sat there in this darkness, and he knew he should've walked away with Steve. He knew he should've gone with him.

But then what would that make him?

Weak.

Father and son, so weak.

He didn't want to walk away.

He didn't want to give up on his desire for revenge against the people who had done this to those he cared about.

Look how far that got you.

He heard that voice in his head. The critical one. And he noticed right then it always had a particular tone to it. A familiar cadence.

It was Dad's voice.

You let your mum down, boy. You're no son of mine. Just a weakling. A little weakling with nothing going for you. No son of mine.

He heard Dad's voice, and he wanted to argue.

He wanted to fight.

He wanted to stand up to him and tell him he was wrong.

He wasn't weak.

He was strong.

But the irony?

The cruel irony?

Dad was right.

He wasn't strong.

He wasn't even strong enough to stand up to him right now.

He could only sit there in the darkness and listen to his dad's voice taunt him.

No son of mine.

No son of mine.

No son of mine.

He sat there in the darkness. He didn't know when he'd next see anybody. If they'd come to feed him or give him water. He didn't know anything anymore.

And as he sat here in total misery... he realised there was a strange comfort to it.

A strange sense that this was where he belonged.

This was exactly where he belonged.

He deserved nothing else.

He closed his eyes, and he took another breath. As deep as he could. Despite his blocked nostrils. Despite his gagged mouth.

He sat there in the darkness, and he thought of Ramiro.

He thought of all the bad things he went through there.

But also the security he had there.

He thought about it all, and as horrible as it was... Billy knew his fate wouldn't be much different to there, after all.

And that was on him.

Because he wasn't strong enough.

Because he was weak.

He felt a tear roll down his face.

Heard his dad's voice condemning him once again.

Boys don't cry, you baby.

Man the fuck up...

He heard those taunts, but he didn't even care about them anymore.

Because this was what he was.

This was who he was.

He felt himself drifting off into more tears.

Into more sadness.

And as he sat there crying in misery, he felt himself giving up completely.

This was where he belonged.

This was all he deserved.

And it was all on him.

CHAPTER THIRTY-SEVEN

Steve walked down the quiet old dual-carriageway by the train tracks, and he wondered where the hell he went from here.

It was a nice day. Proper spring's day. Blue skies. Sound of birdsong. Warm smell in the air. Kind of day that woulda been nice to spend down at the local club with a pint. Didn't have much to do with any of the locals there. Just enjoyed having a drink outside his house. People seemed to judge him less for that. Weird, wasn't it? Drink on your own and you're an alcoholic. Drink the same amount—fuck, *twice* the amount—with a few random folks you don't give a fuck about around you, and you were... well, just a normal bloke?

Yeah. Life was very fucking weird like that.

Or well. It used to be.

Weirdly, things made *more* sense now than they used to.

He looked at the road ahead of him. You get the picture of what these post-apocalyptic roads look like at this stage. The cars were pretty much the trees of the new world. No need to bang on about 'em. Telegraph poles, some of them fallen. Some of them with crows sitting on top of them, staring down. Always the fucking crows, with their beady little eyes. Sneaky bastards, that's what they were.

He looked down at the train tracks beyond the fence beside him. There was a train down there. As stationary and as still as every fucking thing in this wasteland. He wondered how many were on that train when it ground to a halt. How many people rushing back for New Year. How many people going away on work they didn't want to go on. How many kids were stuck on there, expecting to be at their fireworks displays by now, only to be devastated that their train was late.

Damn. How irrelevant it all seemed now.

How irrelevant it all seemed in the grand scheme of things.

He thought about what he was doing on that New Year's Day. On how Kyla came round. Knocked on his door. Told him Oliver was supposed to be back, but he'd been kept away on "work". Work they both knew wasn't really work.

And he remembered seeing her standing there, gorgeous as ever in the moonlight, and feeling so sorry for her. Feeling so fucking sorry for the trap she was in. Trapped with Oliver. Stuck with that evil bastard and unable to do a thing about it.

So he invited her in. Invited her in for a wine. It was a long time since he'd last spoken to her like this. They didn't get much choice nowadays. It was years since their affair. Years since they'd been on one of their little trips abroad together.

He longed for that fairy-tale again. Never did stop loving her. Just wished he could do more. Just wished he could fight for her more.

One of his biggest regrets in life, actually. That he hadn't fought more.

That he hadn't fought for his son more.

He thought about Billy, and he felt sadness, deep inside. An emptiness. He wished he could've done more for that boy. He wished he could've been there for him. He wished he could've had some kind of relationship with him. Some kind of bond with him.

But it wasn't easy. They had a weird setup. An understanding.

An understanding that Billy was Oliver's boy.

And that truth was never to be acknowledged.

Ever.

He thought about the Whistlers.

He thought about the one they called Lucia.

He shuddered.

He hoped to God that boy of his wouldn't see Lucia.

That he wouldn't be forced to meet him.

That he wouldn't be forced to kneel...

But he didn't hold out much hope.

He heard whining by his side. Looked down. Saw Rex, that mutt, right beside him. Unexpected. Never been a big dog person. But hey. He felt like he owed it to Billy. Felt like he owed him that much.

He looked back. Looked over his shoulder. Back to where he'd walked from.

He'd not been there for Billy all these years.

He'd failed him already.

So what had changed now?

What really had changed?

He felt that guilt. That familiar guilt. The one he'd felt so many times, gnawing away at him again.

And he took a deep breath and let it go.

What had changed, really?

What was his choice, really?

What could he do?

Walk back there? Go charging back to the Whistlers? And what then?

He'd die.

Billy would die.

Rex would die.

But...

He looked at Rex again.

At this dog.

At this living reminder of his son.

And he felt that guilt again.

Not hiding away.

Unable to mask it.

And he felt it rising and peaking so, so fucking high.

He stopped.

Stood there.

Looked back.

What was his role in life now?

What was his purpose?

What could he do?

He thought about Billy, and as he stood there, he took a deep breath.

Looked in the direction he knew he had to go—the only way he could go—and he sighed.

"Let's go, mutt," he said.

And then, he walked.

CHAPTER THIRTY-EIGHT

Billy sat in the darkness and wondered when he was finally going to die.

Pitch black again. No sounds again. The taste of blood still in his mouth, as well as sick from the many times he'd choked on that gag. The smell of urine breaking through his blocked nostrils. His own urine, which he was sat in. It was warm when he first let it out. But it was cold now. So cold it made him shiver.

And he didn't want to even think about the shit that was sticking to his body...

He sat there, and he felt so weak. He felt so useless. He just waited. His mouth was dry, and his throat was gasping. He couldn't remember the last time he ate. Couldn't remember the last time he drank. Couldn't remember anything at all. Time had lost all meaning in here. Everything had lost all meaning in here.

It was just a case of waiting now.

Waiting for the end.

It was coming.

It was getting closer.

It was...

A voice.

A voice.

In his head?

No.

It sounded like it was in front of him.

Right in front of him.

He looked up, and he squinted into the darkness. And he knew it didn't make sense. Because he was in the dark. He was in the dark, and it didn't make sense that he'd see anyone at all.

But when he looked ahead, he saw someone standing there.

He saw Aoife standing there.

She was smiling. A big smile on her face.

Or was it... Kayleigh?

He wasn't sure.

But it was one of them.

He saw this Aoife and Kayleigh hybrid, and he heard them say something.

Something he felt like they'd said to him before.

You're strong. You're so, so strong.

You're stronger than you realise.

Stronger than you'll ever realise.

You've made it this far.

You've made it so much further than any of us.

And you're still here.

You're still here.

So remember your promise.

Keep on going.

He heard these words in his head, or outside his head, or all around him.

And then suddenly, it dawned on him.

Suddenly it all made sense.

Suddenly, in a momentary flash, he felt something he hadn't felt for a long time.

For a long, long time.

Energy.

Strength.

He opened his eyes.

He was strong.

He wasn't weak.

He wasn't ever going to give up.

He didn't know how he was going to do it.

He didn't know how he was going to get out of here.

He didn't know anything.

But he did know one thing.

He *was* going to get out of this place.

And he was going to make Sheila pay for what she'd done.

CHAPTER THIRTY-NINE

Sheila worshipped Lucia. She respected Lucia. She adored Lucia. She treated Lucia like a god.

Because Lucia was a god.

But one thing was for sure.

Lucia absolutely terrified her, too.

And that's exactly how it had to be.

It was late. Dark. Pitch black. It'd been a long day. A tiring day. They'd lost people. People of their own. A lot of them had fallen sick after the trip down to the sewers. She knew it was always a risky move. She knew the chance of catching a disease down there was pretty much guaranteed.

But... it was in service of Lucia.

It was in service of Billy.

Because Billy was the key to completing the puzzle.

He was the key to completing *everything*.

And now they had him.

She stood there in this darkened room. The one Lucia resided in.

Lucia's human form that sat on his throne right before her, right now.

The empire he ruled over awaiting him outside.

The boy awaiting him outside.

She sat on her knees on the cold, dusty floor. It was dark in here. Dark but for the moonlight shining in through those huge windows. She could see the pews either side of her. She could see the stain-glass images of Jesus on the windows.

Only Jesus' face had been scratched away. Or smashed away.

And in his place...

Faces.

Faces they'd taken from others.

Faces that represented the outer layer.

Because inside them *all* was Lucia.

The bodies were just a vessel. A conduit.

Lucia was within.

The altar sat right before her. Towered over her. It was absurd to look at. Absurd to see how high he sat in that chair he'd propped above it.

It towered over her.

Towered over everyone.

And in that chair... she saw him.

She saw his silhouette. His darkened silhouette.

She saw his crown.

And she saw the faces alongside him.

His favourite faces.

She looked at him sitting there, and even though she couldn't see his face in the darkness, she knew he was awake.

She knew he was staring at her.

She knew he was waiting for her to tell her exactly what was happening.

Exactly where they were at.

She knelt there on the cold, hard ground. There were no sounds in here. It was peaceful. Churches were always peaceful. Used to always be a place of escape when she was younger. A place of respite. She knew Daddy would never hurt her in the church.

He was a man of God, and he would never lay a finger on her, not in God's house.

He saved that for home.

And as she sat there, heart thumping, face feeling fresh now she'd torn Kaya's face from hers... she felt nervous. Anxious about something. She wasn't sure what exactly. Because she shouldn't be nervous. Today was a good day, after all. Today was a day of celebration. Today was a day they'd been building for, for so, so long.

And yet...

It felt like when you got to Christmas Day. You'd been waiting for it for so, so long. And then suddenly, it was out of the way, and you were back to square one again.

Back waiting for some meaning in your life.

How would Billy's arrival change things in their community?

How would it change Lucia?

She looked up at him, his dark silhouette towering over her, and she swallowed a lump in her throat.

"We have him," she said.

Silence.

Silence but for her own words, echoing around this cold, dark emptiness of the old church.

Silence from Lucia.

"We've had him for... for as long as you told us to keep him. Three days. Three days of silence, just like you said. Just like you prophesied."

More silence.

More staring down at her.

No movement at all from that dark, towering silhouette.

"It's him," she said. "We've... we've absolutely no doubt about it. It's him. He's here. He's right here with us. Waiting. So what... what now?"

More silence.

So much silence that Shelia started to wonder if Lucia was even awake at all.

Even *alive* at all.

And then he moved.

He stood up.

Stood up on that large throne that towered over everybody.

Walked down the altar.

Walked towards Sheila.

Sent a shiver up her spine.

He walked right towards her, and he stopped.

Stopped just before that patch of moonlight.

His face still covered.

And then he stepped into it.

She saw him look down at her.

And she saw him smile.

"It's time," he said.

CHAPTER FORTY

Steve looked down at the Whistlers' camp and wondered what in the name of living fuck he was doing here.

It was early. Sun just rising on the horizon. He could hear the birds singing in the trees. And it might be relaxing if he wasn't about to embark on the most damned pig-headed mission of his entire damned pig-headed life.

Going into the Whistlers' camp.

Sneaking in there.

Getting Billy out of there.

He saw the street beneath him. Pretty normal-looking street by all accounts. Anyone could just wander down here and not know a thing about the place they were walking into. Terraced houses. Old shops boarded up now. And in the distance, a church, looking down over the old market town.

And looking at that church, seeing it... it made him shiver.

He knew what was in there.

He knew *who* was in there.

The one they served.

He remembered when he was one of these people. He remembered how reluctant he was at first. Because of their ways.

Because of their methods. And some of their weird, kooky beliefs didn't add up. But hell, whatever gets people by. They had food. Shelter. And there was a sense of community. It suited Steve just fine for a while.

Then he remembered their discovery of Lucia's "embodied form".

Of Kyla...

He remembered thinking he was dead. That he was finished.

Because the one they claimed was Lucia—the one they claimed was the human vessel of their make-believe god—he despised Steve.

Fucking despised him.

But things were... surprisingly okay. Weird, but okay.

For a while, anyway.

He remembered what happened to Kyla.

Remembered what they did to her.

Remembered being expected to be a part.

To *watch*.

And he remembered walking away.

Sneaking away in the night.

Running away and never looking back.

They came after him. Tried to hunt him down. He hid in empty houses. He hid in old buses. He hid underground in the end, making the sewer his home. So grim down there. You have no idea what it's like being trapped somewhere like that. No daylight. The smell of shit accompanying you all the damned time. You think you'd get used to it eventually. But there ain't no getting used to that.

And standing here now, on this hill, looking down at their home... he knew shit wasn't gonna be easy.

He knew he was walking into a death trap.

But at the end of the day... it was his boy here.

His boy. Whether he called him that or not.

He couldn't just give up on him.

Couldn't just leave him behind.

Especially not after seeing how damned strong he was. How damned tough he was.

He looked down that slope, and he knew he had no choice.

He looked around for the dog. But the dog wasn't here. He'd left him a few miles back. Wrapped a lead around his neck. Nothing too strong. Enough that he'd be able to bite through it if he got absolutely desperate. But enough to stop him following him, too.

And he felt bad. He felt bad that he'd walked away from him. Felt bad at the memory of how Rex barked at him. How he yelped. How he whined.

But the dog had to trust him.

That dog didn't wanna go where Steve was going.

Not for one damned moment.

He took a few deep breaths. Held his knife in hand. His plan was simple. Simple on paper, anyway. But hardly simple in execution.

He was gonna go down into the town via the gardens.

He was gonna go to the old allotments, where he was pretty sure they'd be keeping Billy if he remembered any damned thing about this place.

And then he was going to get him the hell outta there.

He swallowed a lump in his throat.

His heart racing faster and faster.

Still time to turn back, Steve.

Still time to change your mind...

"No," he muttered. "I ain't leavin' him. Not after everythin'."

And then he walked.

The slope down to the little market town was well covered with bushes and foliage. It should block anyone's view of him. Something of a blind spot. He would know. He'd been down this way enough.

The fences stood before him. The fences of the houses on the left side of the main street. He could climb over them. Make his way through them. He'd have to be quick, but if he was quick enough, he could make it to the allotments without attracting too much attention.

He jogged down the slope towards those fences.

You can do this. You can...

A man, up ahead.

Facing away from him. Back to him.

But so close.

Steve froze. Fear jolted right through his veins. Shit. If that bloke saw him, he'd be right onto him. He'd be right onto him, and he'd be whistling.

And he couldn't let him whistle.

Because if he let him whistle... his whole damned game was up.

He crouched down. Crept closer towards that man.

Held his knife tight in his hand.

The man stood there. Right by the fence. He was looking at something. Or... no, *pouring* something against the fence.

It was only when Steve got closer that he realised he was taking a leak.

He shook his head. Saw the piss flooding out of his dick. Flowing fast.

Which meant he still had time.

If he was quick, he could get to him, and...

It all happened so fast.

The man looked around.

He looked right at him.

Held eye contact with him as he kept on pissing for just a few seconds.

Steve froze.

Froze solid, right on the spot, like a rabbit in the headlights.

The man stopped pissing.

He turned around.

Put his piss-wet fingers in his chapped mouth and went to whistle.

Steve bolted towards him, knife raised.

A little whistle crept out of the man's lips.

Steve landed on him.

He buried the knife into his neck.

Covered his mouth.

The man lay back on the floor. Twitching. Shaking free. Desperately trying to break free.

"Quiet," Steve said. "Fucking quiet."

He held the man down. Blood pouring from his neck. His eyes wide, bloodshot. He gargled at Steve. Sounded like he was begging.

But Steve didn't want to fucking hear it.

He waited until the man stopped twitching. Waited until he went still.

Then he looked up at those fences, which reeked of piss.

No whistles.

No whistles at all.

Which meant he still had a chance.

Which meant he was in the clear.

Which meant...

He went to stand when he heard it, clear as day.

A whistle.

Just one whistle, off to his right.

He looked around.

Looked over to the street.

Didn't see a thing.

And then he heard another whistle.

This one to his left.

Fuck.

They were onto him.

They were onto him, and he had to act.

He had to act fast.

He stood up and ran over to the fence. Grabbed the top of it, hauled himself over it. Landed the other side.

Old garden. Barbecue still sitting there on the patio. A kid's bike, pink with white tires, lying on its side. Smashed patio windows, and specks of blood.

And whistling.

More and more whistling.

He stood there, heart racing. He knew he had a decision to make... then realised, no. There wasn't any damned decision to make at all.

He could only go one way now.

He only had one damned choice.

He ran.

Ran to the other side of the garden.

Hauled himself over that fence.

Landed into the next one.

Another whistle.

This one right beside him.

From the house beside him.

He didn't even look this time. He didn't have the time to look.

He just had to keep on going.

He ran as fast as he could across the garden.

Dragged himself up and onto that fence.

Pulled himself to the top of it.

And then he felt it.

A hand.

A hand on his ankle.

Dragging him back down.

Pulling him into the garden.

Losing his balance and tumbling down.

Cracking his head on the solid patio tiles.

He felt sick. His head spun. He could taste blood on his lips.

But he knew he couldn't just give up.

He knew he had to get the fuck up, and he had to fight.

He blinked a few times, and he saw them.

Standing right over him.

Four of them.

Staring down at him.

Faces covered with the masks of the dead.

Flies buzzing around them, reeking of shit.

Knives in their hands.

Smiling.

"Hello, Steve," a voice said.

All the hairs on Steve's body stood right on end.

Hearing that voice.

Hearing it just as clearly as he'd heard it all those years ago.

And still feeling just as terrified by it.

He heard footsteps.

He saw movement.

A figure appearing right before him.

And he saw him looking down at him and smiling.

"Fancy seeing you here," he said. "Just in time for the main event."

CHAPTER FORTY-ONE

Billy didn't know how he would get out of this mess.

But he was *going* to get out. He was going to get the hell out. Even if it was the last damned thing he did.

It was still pitch black, and he still had no idea at all what time of day it was. He had no idea whether it was sunny or cloudy or rainy outside. He had no idea about anything. Anything at all.

Only that he had to get out of here.

He had to get away.

He couldn't sit here and mope.

He couldn't just give up.

He had to try something.

He looked around, even though it was useless. Pitch black. Complete and total darkness as he sat there, blindfolded. That rag at the back of his throat made him want to throw up, made him heave. It tasted so bad, too. Tasted of sick. And he swore he could still smell that nasty sewerage hanging in the air.

It made him feel dizzy. Made him feel sick.

And the binds around his wrists and ankles made him feel trapped, too.

He didn't know how he would get out of this. He didn't know how he would escape.

But he knew one thing.

He wasn't sure how he knew it.

He wasn't sure why he knew it.

But he knew it.

With a deep confidence that came from... well, from nowhere at all, really, he knew it.

He was getting out of here.

This wasn't the end for him.

It wasn't the end.

He pulled at the ties around his wrists. But it was useless. They were so tight. And they dug right into his skin whenever he pulled them too tight. They were stinging like mad. Stinging really, really bad. He knew they were probably cut. He knew they were probably bleeding. Badly.

But what did that matter anyway?

If he didn't try something... he was going to die here anyway.

So what use was giving up?

What use was giving in to the pain?

He pulled harder against those ties. So hard that he could feel them digging in even further to his skin and flesh. Splitting pain. Splitting, searing pain, making him want to scream, making him want to cry out.

But the gag was helping keep him quiet.

The gag that had almost choked him so many times was doing him a favour.

He pulled and pulled, and he thought of Aoife.

Thought of the pain she must've felt when she lost her arm.

He thought of how if they'd got her some medical attention in the old world... maybe she would've made it. Maybe she would've been okay.

He thought about Aoife as those tight, sharp ties dug deeper and deeper into his flesh, and then he felt something.

Right on the verge of giving up, he felt something.

He felt something snap.

Something snap right before him.

He looked down, even though he couldn't see. Heart thumping. Barely able to believe it.

But as he moved his wrists and tried to pull them apart again... he realised something.

The ties.

The ties around his wrists were weaker now.

Looser.

They were coming free.

They were breaking free.

He was almost there.

He pulled against them again.

The pain was awful now. Worse than ever. It felt like a thousand hot knives were being buried into his arms, stabbed into them repeatedly, again and again, and again.

He felt it getting stronger. Felt it getting even more intense. He felt it getting so intense that he started crying.

Give up, Billy. Give up. You're worthless. You ain't anywhere near strong enough. Just do as you're told and give up...

"No," Billy said internally.

He pulled even more.

Pulled against those loosening ties.

He pulled until he couldn't pull anymore.

And then he pulled some more anyway.

His arms shaking.

His body on fire.

I can do this.

I'm not weak.

I can do this.

He felt his wrists splitting and felt blood slithering down his skin.

And then he felt something else.

Heard something else.

A snap.

His wrists came apart.

Slammed back with all the strength he was using.

He sat there. Heart racing. Body shaking. Wrists in absolute agony.

But he felt a smile creep up his face.

He was free.

He pulled the gag out of his mouth, and he heaved everywhere. Vomited burning, acidic bile all over the place.

And then he pulled his blindfold away with his weak, shaking hands, and he saw light.

The room was still dark. But it felt bright compared to before.

He could see he was in some kind of shed. Some kind of big garage or something. There were windows dotted around the room, but they were covered with thick, brown grime, and they were frosted, so it was impossible to see outside.

He looked across the floor of this dirty room, covered in shit and blood, and he saw a door.

A way out.

A way of escape.

He reached down. Grabbed the ties around his ankles. Started to pull at them too with his shaking, shivering hands. As blood pooled from his wrists.

"You can do this," he said. "You're almost there."

He pulled and pulled at the ties.

Pulled as hard as he possibly could.

He wasn't getting trapped here.

He was getting out of here.

He was getting away from here.

He was—

The ties around his ankles came loose.

He was free.

He sat there a few seconds. His heart racing. Tears streaming out of his eyes. A smile across his face as he laughed. He'd done it. He'd actually done it.

Now he just had to get out of this place.

Now, he—

A bang.

A bang on the door.

He looked up.

No. Please no...

The door creaked open.

And the woman walked in.

The one called Sheila.

She stood there with a smile on her face.

"Come on, Billy," she said. "It's time."

Time? Time for what?"

"Lucia will see you now."

CHAPTER FORTY-TWO

Billy barely even had time to process his disappointment at his failed escape.

Because before he knew it, he was being dragged out of the darkness of the room he'd been trapped inside for God knows how long and taken out into the light.

The light that felt more dangerous, somehow.

It was morning, or afternoon, he couldn't really tell. It was sunny. Really sunny. Burning down bright from above. He felt cold, though. Shivery. He could taste blood at the back of his throat, and sharp, burning vomit. His wrists were sore and bloody. He could feel the warm blood trickling down them, down to the ground below.

He could feel something else, too.

Sheila's hard, rough hand against his back.

"Keep walking," she said. "He's been waiting so, so long to see you."

Billy walked. He walked because he didn't have a choice. And he was getting a sense of his surroundings now, too. Getting a sense of the kind of place he was in.

He could see terraced houses either side of him. They looked like the kind of houses he used to live in. Normal. Quiet. Like it was a nice street once upon a time.

The road was cracked and broken. There were a few cars in the street, but unlike most streets, it looked like they'd been moved onto their sides to act as a kind of wall. A series of walls to make it harder for people to break in.

Behind each of those cars, he saw a person.

They were standing there and watching him closely. All of them looked down when he walked towards them. Like they didn't want to see him. Like they didn't want to make eye contact with him.

Like they were scared of him, almost.

He could see something else at the far end of this road. A church. A large, towering church looking over this old market town.

He could see that the spire had been chipped away at a bit like someone had climbed up there and chopped some of it off.

But he could see also that the road led right there, right towards it.

And there were people lining the pavements.

They all looked at him and whispered to one another as they stood there outside the terraced houses, staring.

Looked at him and then lowered their heads when he looked back at them.

It was like they were unsure about him.

Like they were afraid of him.

And he didn't know what to think about that.

He looked around for an escape route. For a path down the side of one of the houses. But they were all terraced, and none of them had little pathways between them.

There were a few shops up ahead. An old bakery and a butcher's next door. He wondered if he could run through there. Run inside and find a way out the back.

But then he felt that hand on his back.

And then he saw the eyes all looking over at him.

And he knew running away wasn't going to be an option.

He was going to meet Lucia, whether he wanted to or not.

He walked further down this street. Every time he stopped or slowed, Sheila gave him a firmer push. And the closer he got to this church—which was clearly where he was heading—he saw more people standing at the side of him.

And these people were wearing the faces of the dead.

These people weren't looking away from him.

These people were watching him.

Closely.

He walked further and further towards the church. He walked through the entrance gate. Past the headstones. He noticed the church windows had been smashed. All the images of Jesus had been torn away. Some of them had been replaced by these faces.

These torn faces of the dead.

It made him shiver.

"Come on," Sheila said. "Almost there."

He didn't want to go any further. He wanted to stay here. He could see those doors to the church waiting before him. Open.

Darkness within.

And as much as he wanted to be strong, he felt scared.

He didn't want to go in there.

Because he feared he might never come out.

"You don't have a thing to worry about," Sheila said. "You are more important to Lucia than anyone."

Billy looked up at her. "I don't... I don't understand."

Sheila looked down at him, and she smiled. "You will. Soon, you will."

Billy looked back at the church doors right in front of him.

He was scared.

So, so scared.

But he took a deep breath.

And then he walked.

He looked back. Looked back at the street. Bathed in sunlight.

They were all looking at him now.

Loads of them.

All staring at him.

All watching.

"Come on," Sheila said. "It's like I said. We're almost there."

Billy swallowed a lump in his throat.

He turned around.

And he walked in through those doors.

And he realised something.

As he walked in, he realised Sheila wasn't right behind him anymore.

She was watching him.

Watching him closely.

But it looked like he was taking these final steps himself.

He swallowed another lump in his throat.

Looked ahead again.

Looked at that darkness within.

Took a deep breath.

"I've got this. I'm strong enough."

He walked through the doors.

The church was quiet. Empty. Cold. It smelled of old people.

Everything echoed around here. Even his breathing. He could see the red pews covered in dust. He could see something red on the floor, too, leading right up to the alter.

Something like blood.

And at the altar, he saw...

There was a man.

A man sitting on a huge chair, right on top of the altar.

He sat there and looked down at Billy.

Sat there and stared at him.

Sat down and smiled.

And Billy was afraid. He was so afraid.

But he couldn't stop himself walking further down that path.

Couldn't stop the feelings he had.

Because there was something about this.

Something wasn't right.

And yet...

Hadn't everything been leading to this?

Hadn't everything been building to this, really?

He walked further down the aisle.

Closer to that man, sitting there on the chair above the altar.

And Billy saw more things, then.

He saw the faces dangling from the windows.

And he saw the body.

The one beside the man on the chair.

No face at all.

Nothing more than a blackened skeleton, now.

But around her, candles.

Around her, pictures.

Around her, photographs.

Photographs of Mum.

Photographs of Dad.

And there was another chair.

A chair to the other side of the altar.

The other side to this man.

And as much as Billy didn't want to face it, as much as he wanted to run from it, as much as he wanted to fight it... he knew exactly who that chair was for.

The man climbed down from the altar.

He stood right in front of it.

He stepped into the light shining through the stained-glass windows.

His face came into view.

The man looked down at him, and he smiled.

"Hello, Billy," he said. "It's been so, so long."

Billy felt fear fill his body.

He felt confusion fill his body.

But he felt something else, too.

A sense of inevitability.

A sense that this was always going to happen.

Because standing before him wasn't someone called Lucia.

Standing before him was someone he knew very well.

Standing before him... was Dad.

CHAPTER FORTY-THREE

"Hello, Billy," Dad said. "It's been so, so long."

Billy stood there and stared up at the man standing before him. It was Dad. He'd walked in here expecting someone called Lucia—someone those people, those Whistlers, worshipped—and instead, he'd found... Dad.

Dad stood before him. Right in the middle of the church aisle. He was wearing such weird clothes. Clothes Dad would never have worn. Like priests' clothes. Robes. Long, white robes, which had patches of brown on them, probably old blood.

On his head, a crown.

And there on his face, a smile.

"It's so, so good to see you again, my boy. So, so good. You have no idea how long I've waited to see you. How long I've waited to see if you'll return. And how proud of you I am. How immensely proud of you I am."

He walked up to Billy. Walked towards him.

And Billy couldn't move.

He couldn't move as Dad reached down and put a heavy hand on Billy's shoulder.

As he squeezed it, just like he always used to squeeze it when

Billy was younger, when he was encouraging him, or when he was happy with him about something.

He couldn't move a muscle.

He could only look up at Dad.

He could only stare.

"I never thought I'd see you again," he said. His voice so firm. No emotion there whatsoever. Like he was performing. Like he was in a play.

Like this wasn't real at all, and all just a performance.

All just a show.

Not the moment he'd waited so, so long for.

He kept on squeezing Billy's shoulder. Holding his hand there, so tight. "There... there were times I thought this day would never come. But now here you are. Here you are, right before me. I am so proud of you, son. I am so, so proud of you."

Hearing those words, Billy had to admit he felt himself drifting off into a haze. They were words he'd wanted to hear Dad say all his childhood. Hearing him say them now... he could almost forget his surroundings. He could almost ignore the circumstances.

But then he pushed himself out of that haze. He looked around.

Looked at the church.

Looked at those faces hanging from the smashed stained-glass windows.

He looked at the chairs either side of the altar.

The one with the body sitting in it.

And then he looked at Dad.

"What... what is this?"

Dad smiled. And then he pulled his hand away, and he walked away. Slowly. Again, like this was all some kind of performance. Not like it was reality. "I fell upon this place rather accidentally, in all truth. I—I was searching for you, my boy. Searching and searching and searching. I didn't find you. But Sheila. Her people.

They found *me*. And there was a need for strength. There was a need for unity. The idea of the old community... it died with the old world. But when I found these people. When I found Sheila. When I found out I was a disciple of Lucia and that I was the real *embodiment* of Lucia... I realised how different things could really be."

Billy shook his head. "I—I don't understand."

"You wouldn't," Dad said. "Because you haven't been exposed to our teachings yet. You haven't lived through what we've lived through. But you will. You absolutely will. And when you do... you'll take a seat on the throne next to me. And you will follow me. And *you* will be the embodiment of Lucia. You are the son of Lucia."

Billy didn't know what to say or what to think. Only that he had a bad feeling in his stomach. In his chest. Because this wasn't the Dad he remembered. This man was... crazy. He was clearly out of his mind.

He looked around. He had to find a way out of here. He had to escape, somehow.

The church door he'd walked in through was blocked now. People were standing there. People with the faces of the dead wrapped around theirs.

Sheila stood at the front of them, staring at Billy.

Smiling.

Dread filled Billy's body. The door was blocked. Dad was insane. He'd lost his mind.

And he wasn't going to get out of this place.

He looked back around. Back at Dad.

And then at that body on the chair beside his altar.

Beside his throne.

"What... What happened to her, really?"

Dad narrowed his eyes. "To whom?"

"To... to Mum."

Dad's face dropped. For a moment, the performance slipped

away, and Billy saw sadness in his eyes. Pure sadness. "I... Your mother was a lovely woman. The love of my life. But she committed a sin. A sin so great it required... adequate sacrifice."

Billy burned up with hatred. Hatred for his own dad. "You—you killed her?"

"I freed her."

"You killed her!" Billy shouted.

Dad jumped. Flinched, just for a moment. And he looked scared.

And Billy felt a lifetime of anger at his dad bubbling up inside and peaking high than ever.

He'd killed Mum.

He'd killed Kayleigh.

And now here he was. Leader of whatever the hell this group was.

Completely out of his mind.

"You show a rare anger, Billy," Dad said. Smiling. "A... a strength. Look at you. All grown up. I always knew you'd grow into a strong man. Especially after you got away from your mother's clutches."

Rage burned through Billy's body. He went to throw himself at Dad. "Don't you dare—"

And then he felt someone stop him.

Someone holding him back, stopping him going any further.

And Dad just stood there, smile on his face. Looking proud. "Really. I am so, so happy to see what you've grown into. I can't even begin to explain."

He turned around, then. Walked right back down the aisle, back towards his altar.

"But now you have a choice to make, my boy," he said. "An opportunity to prove who you really are. To prove you are my son. To prove you are heir to Lucia. Once and for all."

A gut feeling of dread in the pit of Billy's chest. What was he talking about? What choice?

Dad walked up to the altar. And then he stroked the face of the skeleton sitting on that chair. "I love you, Kyla. I always will love you. And now it's time to see just how strong our boy really is."

Billy felt sick. He shook his head, tried to break free of the hands holding him in place. But he felt weak. And he felt dizzy. And he felt like he couldn't do this. He just couldn't do this...

"Bring him out, Sheila. Bring him before us. Then the boy understands exactly what he has to do to prove himself."

A bang.

Struggling, right behind Billy.

And then footsteps.

Billy looked around.

Sheila walked towards him.

She dragged someone along with her.

Someone who had a bag over his head.

A leash around his neck.

He was trying to fight free, but he wasn't doing a very good job.

"Bring him right here. Right before us all."

Sheila walked past Billy.

She walked past him, dragging this man along.

She walked until she was in the light shining in through the broken windows, at the feet of the altar, at the feet of Lucia's throne, and of Dad himself... and she stopped.

Dad smiled. "Thank you, Sheila. I'll take it from here."

Sheila walked away. And Dad looked up at Billy. He looked up at him as he stood behind this man, who sat on his knees, right before him. Facing Billy.

"You have a chance," Dad said. "An opportunity to prove you are my son. An opportunity to prove you are the future. That you are the embodiment of Lucia."

He put his hand on the sack on the man's head.

Billy's heart raced.

He couldn't move a muscle.

He couldn't speak.

"You can prove yourself by making a sacrifice," Dad said.

And then he lifted the sack away.

Steve knelt before him.

His face was purple and bruised. He was bleeding badly. He looked like he'd beaten up. Real bad.

Dad stood right behind him. Knife in hand.

And he looked at Billy, and he smiled.

"You must sacrifice this man," he said. "You must sacrifice this traitor. This apostate. This false idol. This devil. And you must do it for your family. You must do it for Lucia. You must do it for your father."

CHAPTER FORTY-FOUR

Billy saw Steve kneeling before him, and he knew with absolute certainty that one of his dads was going to die today.

He stood in the middle of the church aisle. The pews beside him were empty. But the door to the church was blocked. His way out was blocked by so many people.

All staring at him.

All waiting to see what he did.

Waiting to see how he acted.

Waiting to see whether he really was their "heir to the throne."

And he felt sick. He felt scared. He felt angry. He felt emotions stronger than he'd ever felt them before.

Because... Dad.

Dad had killed Mum.

He'd killed Mum, and now he was in some crazy cult.

And there was Steve.

There was Steve. The man who claimed he was Billy's real dad.

On his knees.

His face looked battered and bruised. He was covered in blood. His eyes were all swollen, and his lips were full of cuts.

He looked right at Billy. Stared right at him. Didn't say a word.

Almost like he expected this moment to arrive.

And Billy didn't know what to do, seeing him sitting there. He didn't know how to think.

Because this was the man who was supposedly his dad.

His real dad.

And this *other* dad was asking him to kill him.

To sacrifice him.

"I know what I'm asking you to do is rather crude," Dad said. Walking around from side to side. Pacing. And speaking in those performative tones, once again. Like this was all a show he was putting on for his people.

Not the reunion Billy expected.

Not the reunion with his father that he'd hoped and prayed so, so much for.

"But you are my boy. And you have a chance to prove it. For real."

He nodded at someone just out of sight. Billy thought it was at him at first.

But then someone handed him a knife.

Planted him a long, curved blade, right into his hands.

"You will kill him," Dad said. "You will make this sacrifice. Because you have to. If you do not… then there is no other option than for you to take a seat beside your mother. And not in the way you want to. Not in the way any of us want you to."

Billy felt like he was dreaming. Like this was some kind of horrible nightmare. He wanted to ask Dad, why? Why had he done what he'd done? Where had things gone so wrong for him to end up like this? He'd never been nice to Billy. But he was Dad. And he loved him. They loved each other.

He shook his head. "It's me, Dad. It's… it's me." He didn't know what else to say. "It's me."

Dad looked back at him. That performative expression dropping from his face again, for just a second. Like he was in a battle. A battle with himself.

And then that smile arose again. "I know who you are, Billy. My Billy. But you have to prove it. That's exactly what you have to do. Right now."

Billy shook his head. "Steve told me—"

"You do not say his name!" Dad exploded.

Billy jolted back. That old sense of fear he'd felt around Dad returning again.

His eyes were so red. So bloodshot.

He looked mad.

Like he could snap and kill everyone in this church at any moment.

And then he smiled again. Laughed a little. "My apologies. But I do feel very, very strongly about this. It's an emotional moment for all of us, isn't it? It's very hard to keep a sense of composure all the time."

Billy felt himself calming down after that bolt of anger. But still... seeing this man he used to call Dad. Seeing this man he used to go on holidays with. Seeing this man he used to play on the Xbox with... he felt like his whole world was tearing apart. Splitting into two.

He'd just wanted this man to be proud of him.

All his life, he'd just wanted to be good enough in his eyes.

And now look at him.

Now look what he was.

"I can't do this," Billy said.

Dad stopped pacing. He narrowed his eyes, standing there right by Steve's side. "What did you just say?"

Billy felt ashamed. A familiar sense of shame and weakness, all over again. He lowered his head. "I can't... I can't just kill him."

Footsteps.

Footsteps powering down the aisle towards him.

He looked up.

Dad was marching towards him.

A look of anger in his eyes.

Like when Billy didn't want to go on the rollercoaster at Blackpool with him that time.

He'd shouted at him so much for that.

His body tensed up.

He felt himself inching away like that scared little boy again.

And then Dad grabbed him.

Grabbed him by his bleeding right arm.

Yanked him forward.

"You will kill him," he said. "You will kill him. You won't fail me. You won't fail my people. Not after all this time."

Billy tried to move away, tried to flee, but it was no use. Dad dragged him along the aisle.

Dragged him until he reached Steve.

Dragged him until he was standing right in front of him.

Steve stared up at Billy. He wasn't begging. He wasn't trying to say anything. He wasn't shaking, and he didn't look afraid.

He just knelt there and looked into Billy's eyes.

Dad put his hands on Billy's shoulders.

He leaned into his ear.

"I know I wasn't always the most encouraging father," he said. "I know I was always... critical. But I see your strength now. I see it in your eyes, Billy. Don't fail me now. Please don't fail me now. Prove your strength. Prove you're my boy."

And hearing those words.

Hearing those words made Billy *want* to prove himself to Dad.

To prove himself like he'd never been able to, all those times, for all those years.

"Prove yourself."

Billy looked down at the knife in his hand.

"Prove you're as strong as I know you are."

He shook his head. Closed his eyes. Took a deep breath.

Dad squeezed his shoulders. "Prove you're my boy."

And then Billy opened his eyes.

He looked at Steve.

He swallowed a lump in his throat.

"I'm sorry," he said. "I have to. I have to."

And then he pulled back the knife.

CHAPTER FORTY-FIVE

Billy closed his eyes, held his breath, and swung the knife.

He didn't want to open his eyes. He didn't want to look at what he'd just done. He didn't want to *see*.

Because he could see it in his mind already, clear enough.

Steve's face.

Steve's bloodshot eyes widening as he buried that knife into his chest.

The deep crimson blood pooling out of him, all warm on his hand.

He thought about the approval in his dad's eyes. The smile on his twisted face and how sick it made Billy feel.

Because for the first time in his life... Billy realised he didn't want it.

He didn't want Dad's approval.

Not in this way.

He opened his eyes, and he looked ahead.

Steve knelt there before him. His eyes were swollen and bruised. There were cuts and scratches all over his tired, grey, dishevelled face. He looked up at Billy with wide eyes. Stared up at him. Was that shock on his face?

And Billy felt it, then. He felt the warm blood oozing out onto his hand.

He heard the gasping.

And as he stood there, he knew this was inevitable.

He knew this was the only way things could go.

But that blood.

That blood wasn't coming from Steve.

It was coming from someone else.

He looked around and saw Dad standing there, holding on to his chest.

He was bleeding. Badly. He looked down at the wound where Billy had buried the knife. Blood painted his off-white robes red. And that red patch was spreading, faster and faster.

He clutched those robes with his shaking fingers. Behind him, by the entrance to the church, his people looked on. Some of them were frowning. Some of them were wandering over. Some of them were smiling like they didn't even realise what had happened.

"Why?" Dad muttered. Holding his bleeding chest with both his shaky hands now. He looked down at Billy, that crown dangling loosely from his head. And he didn't look angry. He didn't even look surprised anymore.

Mostly, he looked... sad.

"I'm your dad," he said. "I'm... I'm your dad and... and you were supposed to be strong. You were—you were supposed to be my son. You were supposed to be... to be the heir. To me. To... to Lucia. To all of this."

Billy stood there, heart racing. He felt like he was hanging in a cloud of shock. Like this wasn't real. Like he hadn't just done what he'd just done.

He'd stabbed him.

He'd stabbed his own dad in the chest.

He'd spent so, so long trying to find him, and now he'd found him, he'd stabbed him.

Dad stumbled towards Billy. Limped towards him like a zombie from one of his old games. Behind him, in this cold, echoey church, more of his people looked on with shocked faces. "I... I spent so long trying to... trying to raise you right. And then... and then trying to find you again. And now... and now..."

He stopped.

Stopped right in front of Billy.

Stood there and wobbled backwards and forwards like a jack in a box.

There were tears in his eyes.

Blood on his chin.

He was getting paler and paler by the second.

"Why? You were... you were supposed to be strong. Why?"

Billy took a deep breath.

"I *am* strong," he said. "I've always *been* strong."

He pulled back his knife again and buried it into this man's chest.

Dad let out a wince. More blood spurted out over Billy. He opened his mouth to speak, opened his mouth to say something. But then blood just drooled out of his lips, down his chin.

"You were never a dad to me," Billy spat. "And after what you've done to Mum... after what your people did to Kayleigh... you never will be."

Dad narrowed his eyes. More tears trickled out. His blood-drenched lips began to quiver as he tried to speak.

"My son," he said. "My... my boy."

And Billy felt bad.

He felt bad because, for a second, he saw the dad he *had* loved.

He saw the dad he admired.

The dad he was so, so keen on impressing.

So, so eager to live up to.

He saw him for a moment.

And then Dad fell to the church floor.

Slammed face-first against the aisle.

A puddle of blood billowed out underneath him, growing like a disease.

Billy stood there and looked down at him. Looked down at this man lying here beneath him.

A man he used to respect.

A man he used to love.

He looked down at him lying there, twitching, occasionally gasping and choking for breath.

And then he heard the screams.

He looked up.

The people.

Dad's people.

Lucia's people.

They were losing their shit.

Some of them were crying.

Some of them looked furious.

And some of them...

Some of them were slitting their own wrists.

Cutting their own throats.

"Not Lucia! Our dear Lucia!"

A shiver crept up Billy's spine. He still couldn't believe what'd just happened, what he'd just done. But he didn't have time to stick around here.

He had to get away from here.

He turned around and ran.

Looked around the church.

Looked for a way out.

Looked for an escape.

The stained-glass windows staring down at him.

A brown door, over to the left-hand side.

He had to go through there.

He had to try and find a way out through there.

It was his only option.

He ran over towards that door when something suddenly struck him.

Steve.

Steve was still kneeling there before him.

Still gagged.

Still cuffed around his wrists.

Staring back towards that manic, screeching oncoming crowd with fear.

Billy grabbed his hands with his blood-soaked fingers. Pulled him up. Yanked his gag away. "You need—we need to go."

Steve rose to his feet with him. But he wasn't moving quickly enough.

Those footsteps were racing closer towards them both.

They were coming.

They were closing in.

"Steve," he said. "We need—we need to go."

Steve moved a little quicker now. Still not quick enough for Billy's liking. Especially not with the chaos approaching from behind.

The bodies tumbling over the pews.

The shouting.

The screams.

It was terrifying.

Filled him with absolute terror.

"Come on," he said.

The door was right ahead now.

He could go through there.

Go through there and find a way out of here.

Find an escape route.

"Almost there," he said. "Almost..."

He grabbed the door handle.

Turned it.

It opened right before him.

He stepped through the door when he noticed something.

Steve.

Steve had stopped.

"Steve?" Billy said.

Steve stood there in the church doorway. The light from the smashed stained glass window above him shone down through it, casting a glow over him. An angelic glow.

He looked at Billy, and he smiled.

Smiled as that swarming mass got closer to him.

"Go to Brook Street," Steve said. "You'll find that dog of yours there."

"Steve?"

"I'll do what I can to hold 'em back. But right now... you need to go, Billy. Ain't no time to debate about it. Ain't no time to argue about it. You need to go."

No. He wasn't leaving him. Not after everything. Not another loss. He shook his head. "I'm not leaving you behind."

"You don't have a choice," Steve said. "You don't have the luxury of time, kiddo. Go. Get yourself the hell away from here. And don't you forget how strong you are, kid. Don't you... don't you ever forget that."

A lump swelled in Billy's throat. He shook his head. "Steve—"

"I'm sorry, lad," Steve said. "I'm sorry I couldn't be better for you while you were growin' up. I guess this is my way of apology, huh?"

Billy stood there, totally still.

He stared at Steve.

Stared at this man who loved Mum.

This man who was his dad.

His biological dad.

And then he shook his head again. "I can't..."

Then he saw them.

The masses.

So close now.

So close to surrounding Steve.

So close to the door.

Steve smiled. Rolled his eyes. "Just another twist in this crazy life, huh? Now go. You go on and live yours. And you don't look back. Understand? You don't fuckin' look back for anythin'."

Billy felt like he'd been punched in the gut.

He didn't want to turn his back on Steve.

He didn't want to run away from this man who was his real father.

He didn't want any of that.

But as he stood there, and as those crazy cultists approached, he knew he didn't have a choice.

He knew there was only one option.

"Go live your life as best you can," Steve said. "And go get that dog of yours on the way. 'Cause he's a good'un."

Billy wanted to say so much to Steve.

He wanted to say so many things to him.

But in the end, he knew he didn't have a choice.

He had to be strong.

He had to be that strong person he'd never believed he was.

And sometimes being strong meant letting go.

"I'm sorry," Billy said.

Steve smiled. Gaps between those yellow teeth on show. "No, *I'm* sorry. I'm sorry I only just now got to know you. 'Cause yer a fuckin' star, lad. A fuckin' star. And you're a credit to your mother. Now go."

Billy wanted to stay here.

He wanted to hug Steve.

He wanted to give up alongside him.

But he knew there was no choice.

He looked at Steve. Into his eyes. Once more.

And for a second, for just a second, he saw himself looking into a mirror.

A mirror image of himself when he was older, staring back at him.

He looked into his eyes, and he smiled at him through the tears.

And then, as the crowd descended, he slammed the door shut, and he ran.

CHAPTER FORTY-SIX

Billy didn't look back once.

Just as Steve told him.

It was late in the day. Dark and dismal. He'd been walking for God knows how long now. He was on another street of terraced houses. It was empty, and it was quiet. A lot of the windows were boarded up, but those boards had been pulled and hacked away at. One of the houses had graffiti smeared right across it—"GOVT 666: RESIST". The door looked like it'd been bashed in long ago, the grass almost as tall as the front window. Another story that Billy wouldn't hear the ending of.

He walked down the middle of this street. Even though it was quiet, he kept on hearing movement. Shuffling, between the abandoned cars, with their smashed windows. He walked past one and saw a booster seat in the back, a cot beside it. A little SpongeBob teddy being gnawed at by bugs. He wondered where the owner was now. Whether they'd made it.

He got a feeling he didn't really want to know the answer.

The air smelled like a storm. Like a torrential storm on a warm day. That nice earthy smell. Dad used to say it was called something. Something beginning with "p". But Billy couldn't remember what it was now.

Dad...

He felt the sticky, hard blood all over his hands, and he thought back to that moment.

The moment he'd buried the knife into his chest.

The moment he'd chosen Steve over him.

And the more he thought about it, the sicker he felt. The dizzier he felt. The more his breathing picked up, and he felt like he was going to hyperventilate and pass out and...

Deep breaths in.

In through the nose... out through the mouth. In through the nose... out through the mouth.

You're strong.

You've got this.

You're strong.

He heard shuffling beside him. Whimpering.

When he looked down, he saw Rex walking along with him.

Rex was in a mood with him. He wouldn't look him straight in the eye. He had his head lowered, and he wasn't wagging that little docked tail like usual.

Sulker. Absolute sulker. When Billy found him, when he went to where Steve told him he'd left him, he saw him sitting there, tied to the tree. He barely even acknowledged him when he got there. Definitely giving him the cold shoulder.

But he was here now. And he would come around.

They'd get through this.

They'd both get through this.

He walked on further down this cracked and abandoned road. Past an old barber. Past an old newsagent. All of them boarded up. All of them empty. Everything so silent and so empty and so dead.

And he had no idea where he was going to go now.

He had no idea what his direction in life was anymore.

He didn't know what he was going to do. Or where life was going to take him.

But he was strong.

He had to keep telling himself he was strong.

He had to keep believing he was strong.

He thought about Dad. He thought about the good times growing up. The times they'd kicked the football to one another in the garden. The time Dad had been so proud of him when he'd finally learned how to ride a bike. The times they sat on the beach together and talked about Halo and Forza until they were blue in the face.

But then...

Even though that was the past, there was darkness there. There was a side to him Billy didn't want to think about.

That he didn't want to admit.

A darkness.

He swallowed a lump in his throat and looked down at that blood smeared across his hands.

Whatever happened... Dad wasn't Dad anymore.

He'd completely gone.

He didn't want to turn back. Didn't want to look. Just as Steve told him.

But he wondered how far behind those people were.

His cult.

He wondered whether they'd stop chasing. There were a lot of them. And he didn't really want to run into them again.

He looked down at Rex instead of looking around.

Saw him finally making eye contact with him.

Finally, wagging that tail.

"Cheered up now, huh?"

Rex nudged his leg with his head.

And it made a lump swell in Billy's throat.

Made him smile.

And cry a little.

"We'll be strong," he said. "You and me... we're ready for anything. We have to be ready for anything. We—"

He tumbled forward. A loose manhole cover sent him falling to his feet.

He lay there, felt the pain.

And he bit his lip.

He tensed through the tears.

We'll be strong.

He pushed himself back to his feet, resisting crying, resisting the urge to give up, and he took a deep breath.

"Let's go, Rex," he said. "Let's—"

"Not another move."

A voice.

A voice right behind.

The hairs on Billy's neck stood on end.

His stomach sank.

That voice.

He'd heard that voice before.

That familiar voice.

He turned around slowly.

Sheila was standing there.

And she was holding someone.

Someone kneeling before her.

Knife to his neck.

Steve.

She looked at Billy with tears rolling down her angry face.

A snarl.

"This ends," she said. "This ends, *now*."

CHAPTER FORTY-SEVEN

"It's over, Billy. It's all over."

Billy stood there in the pouring rain. The grey sky above just kept on getting greyer and greyer, darker and darker. Took him back to his favourite weekends as a kid. The weekends where it wasn't sunny were always best. Because it meant there'd be no real pressure for him to go out and play with other kids. A grey weekend meant a weekend inside, playing on his video games. Just how he liked it.

But right now, it felt different.

Steve was on his knees before him, right in the middle of the road. Sheila stood behind him. A knife to his throat. She had an angry look on her face. Looked mad. Real mad.

"It's over, Billy," she repeated. "No point keeping fighting like this. No point persisting. Just accept your fate, and it'll be easier for you. It'll be easier for everyone."

Billy felt his stomach sink. He'd been so naive to think he'd made it. So stupid to think he was on his own and that Lucia's followers—his dad's followers—wouldn't have been following him.

But seeing Steve alive here... that was a surprise.

That was something he wasn't expecting.

He remembered the last time he'd seen him.

Standing at that door in the church.

Lucia's followers swarming from behind.

The way he looked into Billy's eyes, and he smiled.

"Run. Run and don't look back."

"You're stronger than you know."

And then Billy turned around, and he ran.

Ran and didn't stop running until he was absolutely sure there was nobody behind him.

But seeing him here, seeing that he was still alive, and seeing he had another chance... that awoke something inside him.

"You did well, getting away like you did," Sheila spat. "When Lucia said you were strong, we never really realised just *how* strong he meant. But taking him down. Taking him down like you did... you should be finished for what you did. For the pain and suffering you've caused."

He could hear something in her voice. Something that sounded... desperate. Fearful.

Like she was afraid of him.

"Let him go," Billy said.

Sheila smiled. Laughed. Shook her head. Pulled that blade closer to Steve's throat. Held it so tight against it that Steve struggled to breathe. "You just don't get it, do you? We can never forgive you for what you've done. For destroying our dear leader. You'll be hunted down by our people for the rest of your short and miserable life."

"I'll take my chances."

"But," Sheila said, "there is another way."

Another way? What the hell was she talking about?

Even after he'd done what he'd done?

Even after he'd killed his own father?

The guy they worshipped like a god?

"What other way?"

Sheila's smile widened. She laughed a little. Sounded nervous. "I thought you'd never ask."

She looked down at Steve as he knelt there before her, then. His neck was bleeding now. His face was cut and bruised even worse than before, and he looked like he'd had ten shades of shit kicked out of him.

"At first," she said, moving that blade softly across his neck, "I thought your act was an act of the Devil."

She kept on moving that blade across his neck.

Slicing his skin like it was butter.

More blood trickling and oozing out down onto his sodden grey shirt.

"I thought it was an act of betrayal. An act of hatred."

She stopped moving the blade, and she looked right up at Billy.

"But now I see things very differently. Very differently indeed."

Billy frowned. What the fuck was she on about?

"Now... I see you are Lucia. You are the true Lucia. The son of our former leader. Our former god. And you have a chance. You have a chance to take your throne. To sit right where your father sat and rule."

What the hell was this woman talking about? He didn't know what to say. Didn't know what to think. One thing was abundantly clear. These people were crazy. They believed whatever they wanted to believe. And now they were actually choosing to believe he might be some kind of god, too?

Billy cleared his throat. "I don't quite understand."

"You made your sacrifice," she said. "You chose to murder your own father. *That* is strength. Sheer strength."

Billy felt sick. He didn't want to think about what happened with Dad. He didn't want to think about any of it. He took a few deep breaths, tried to cool himself down. "What do you want?"

"Join us," she said. "Come back home and take your seat on

the throne. Or I'll... I'll be forced to finish what you couldn't finish and take the throne for myself."

Billy shook his head. "I still don't understand—"

"Steve here," she said. "Steve here will die if you do not comply."

A knot in Billy's stomach.

"Your father. Your *true* father. Dead. Blood on your hands. Is that what you want?"

"Don't listen to her bullshit, Billy."

Sheila punched him across the back of the head. Hard.

Knocked him down to the road with surprising force.

"You shut that traitor mouth of yours," she said. Then she spat on him.

She looked back at Billy. Her blue eyes seemed to illuminate. "You join me. You return home. And sure. There will be punishment for what you did. For the sin you committed. But I can root for you. I can be on your side. I've seen the power you have in yourself. I've seen who you really are and what you're capable of. And you can have that. You can have all of it. You just need to join me."

"I'll never fucking join you," Billy said. "Not after the things you've done."

Sheila's face dropped. She pulled that knife to Steve's throat again. "I strongly suggest you change your mind."

"Go, Billy," Steve said. Staring at him with those tired, bloodshot eyes. "Remember what I said. Never look back. Never—"

Sheila pulled the knife closer to Steve's neck.

Sliced his skin again, opening another small wound, which trickled down onto his shirt.

"I already told you," she said. "Quiet. I do not want to hear another word from you. Understand?"

Billy stood there, frozen. What could he do? Walk away? Walk away and leave Steve here? Leave his real *dad* here, after everything he'd done?

Or do something about it?

Stand up?

And prove his strength?

No. Not *prove* his strength.

He didn't *have* to prove his strength to anyone. Especially not anymore.

He just had to *be* strong.

Because it was the right thing to do.

"Go, Billy!" Steve shouted. "Don't dick around here. Just —just go!"

Another slice against his neck.

"One more chance to shut the hell up, or I slit his throat."

Billy's heart raced.

His chest tightened.

He could barely breathe.

You've got this.

You're strong.

You know what the right thing to do is here.

He took a deep breath.

"Wait here, Rex," he said.

And then he walked.

He walked along the road. Walked towards Sheila. Walked towards Steve.

Sheila smiled. "That's it. That's exactly it."

"Billy..." Steve said.

Billy kept on walking.

Fists clenched.

Gaze firmly set on Sheila.

Right into her eyes.

He walked down the street until he was just inches in front of her, and he stopped.

Sheila was silent. She didn't say anything. Just looked down at him and smiled.

And then eventually, she said: "Well?"

Billy looked at Steve.

Steve stared back at him, shaking his head. "Don't do this."

Billy took a deep breath and looked back up at Sheila. "What do I need to do?"

Sheila's smile widened. Her eyes widened. And right then, Billy realised from the mere look on her face that she was a lost cause, too. She was crazy, too. Well. He knew it anyway. But he never really realised just how far gone she was.

Believing him.

Believing that he was actually laying down his arms.

Unless...

"I'll tell you what you need to do," Sheila said.

She pulled back her knife and stabbed Steve in his shoulder.

Then she pushed him aside as he cried out in pain.

"You need to know when you're defeated."

She pulled back her knife.

Billy stepped back.

Stepped right over that manhole cover, the one he'd tripped on before.

And just as Sheila launched towards him, he kicked the edge of the manhole cover up, right into Sheila's path.

Sheila tumbled.

She lost her balance.

Fell face flat onto the road.

Her knife fell from her grip.

Billy didn't hesitate.

He grabbed her knife.

Then he grabbed her hair.

Looked her in those blue eyes.

"I'll never kneel for you monsters," he said. "And that's the difference between us. I know what's right. I know what I'm fighting for."

And then he buried the knife into Sheila's throat.

She opened her mouth. Squirmed. Choked on the blood.

And Billy looked into her eyes at all times as she gasped, as she spluttered, as she tried to say something, anything, tried to speak...

And then he pulled the knife away and let her fall to the road.

He watched her struggle. He watched her battle for life. And as he watched her, he felt sorry for her, in a way.

The woman who'd killed his mum.

The woman who'd killed Kayleigh.

The woman who'd made an unstable, deranged Dad a god-like figure in her crazy cult.

He felt sorry for her.

He watched her open her mouth. Watched blood bubble out from her chapped lips.

He watched her blue eyes widen, staring up at him.

"Weak..." she said. "Weak..."

He felt it. Felt that word sting.

The word people screamed at him his entire life.

Then he exhaled.

He wasn't weak.

He was strong.

Far, far stronger than he'd ever believed.

He watched Sheila's eyes widen one more time, all bloodshot and red.

He watched her reach out a shaking hand in his direction.

He watched her try to say something.

And then he saw her go still.

"Fuckin' hell, that hurts," a voice said.

Billy looked around.

Steve was lying on the road.

Bleeding from his shoulder.

Badly.

Billy walked over to him.

He reached his side. Knelt down beside him. "It's okay. I'm— I'm here. It's over. It's okay."

Steve clutched his bleeding shoulder. He was still bleeding a little from the neck, too. "You should've just run," he said. "You shoulda just done as you were damned told."

"But then you'd be gone," he said.

He helped Steve to his feet. Held on to him, even though Steve was taller and bigger than him.

He looked over at Sheila, who lay there. Still twitching. Still choking. Still clawing out her shaking hand like she was reaching out for life.

"We should get away from here. Before... before the rest of them catch up. You okay?"

Steve looked down at him. Holding his bleeding neck now, too. Staring at him with wide eyes. "You really are a tough bastard, ain't ya?"

Billy swallowed a lump in his throat. And he wasn't sure why he said it or where it came from, but he found himself saying something he didn't expect. "I guess... I guess I take after my dad."

Steve laughed a little, which made him wince. "Nah. You're far, far tougher than him."

"I mean you."

They stood together.

Stood there with Rex.

Stood in the middle of the street as the rain stopped, and a single ray of sunlight broke through the clouds, bathing them in light.

They didn't say a word. Just stood there and stared together.

That unspoken understanding of who they were hanging in the air between them.

"Where now?" Steve said.

"What?"

He cleared his throat. "I mean... I mean, I'm stabbed, and I'm beaten, and I'm bleeding like hell. A crazy cult might just be on our damned tail. You got any bright ideas in that brain of yours, huh?"

Billy looked at Steve. Then at Rex. Then at the street around him. This world he'd grown up in. This world he'd adapted to. This world he knew better than any other.

He looked at this world he thought he was afraid of. This decaying world. This dying world.

He thought about all the horrors in it.

He thought about the awful people he'd come across.

The nightmarish encounters.

Ramiro.

Carlton.

Sheila.

His own father...

And then he thought of something else.

The good people.

People like Aoife.

People like Kayleigh.

People like Steve.

He took a deep breath.

He swallowed a lump in his throat.

"We'll find a way," he said.

Steve smiled back at him. "Yeah. Yeah, I guess we will."

Billy looked down at Rex. He crouched beside him. Stroked his soft head. "You're a good lad. You know that? You're such a good lad. And I'm so happy you're here with me."

Rex licked his face, slobbering all over him.

Billy laughed. Tumbled back a little. Saw Rex wagging his tail. And he felt himself welling up. Felt a tear tricking down his face.

He tried to resist it. Tried to stop it.

And then he just let that tear fall.

Crying didn't make him weaker.

Nothing made him weaker.

He'd proven he was strong by being here.

He'd proven he was strong to himself so many times.

He was finally beginning to see it.

He kissed Rex's fur. Tasted the remnants of that sewage and almost heaved right there on the spot.

Then he got back up.

Stood by Steve's side.

Steve didn't look well. He looked pale. The bleeding on his shoulder was bad. Seeping between his fingers. He needed it seeing to immediately.

He felt all these worries building up, all these worries growing, and then he exhaled again and let them go.

"We'll find a way," he said.

And then together, they walked along the road.

Towards the future.

Towards a new beginning.

Towards a new start.

Together.